"There is a zestful Ru
and approach which
of Insects is full of a

"*The Life of Insects*, Pelevin's new novel, takes a Каrкас...   е
and kneads it, logically. . . . Pelevin's lovely novelty is that he com-
bines the hard, allegorical satire of Kharms and Mayakovsky with
a mournful tenderness for ordinary Russians and their ordinary
predicaments that sometimes recalls Chekhov. . . . As a surrealist,
he makes explicit, obvious political arguments; but as a novelist, he
summons deeper, buried significances. . . . *The Life of Insects* is in
deep communion with the Chekhovian dialectic of loss and freedom.
. . . In Chekhov, as in much Russian fiction, characters long to fly. By
giving his characters wings almost too fragile to use, Pelevin makes
good on that longing, but with tender irony."
—James Wood, *Bookforum*

"A shimmering satire of post-Perestroika Russian society . . . Pelevin
pulls off a delicate magical realist balancing act: he simultaneously
builds believable characters with real human struggles, matches their
personality quirks to vivid insect lives, and wittily spoofs various
aspects of Russian culture and international literature. . . . Inventive,
lyrical, and playfully philosophical, *The Life of Insects* luridly projects
the complexities of human life onto the sparkling strangeness of the
insect world."   —*The Boston Phoenix*

"Pelevin's exceptional new novel defies critical comparisons, existing
on its own extraordinary terms. . . . Like Kafka's *Metamorphosis*, *Life*
operates on various metaphoric and allegorical levels. And just when
you think you've located a center of meaning in the novel, he diverts
your attention with yet another startling development."
—*Time Out New York*

"[A] witty satire . . . commenting on the tumultuous quality of
contemporary Russian life, Pelevin uses Gogolian wit and tempers it
with a Bulgakovian belief in the integrity of his characters. Even
root-chewing, dung-eating insects have aspirations and make choices
they hope will improve their lives. Pelevin's is a powerful voice of
Russian absurdism that has broken out of the Soviet rubble."
—*Publishers Weekly*

PENGUIN BOOKS

LIFE OF INSECTS

Victor Pelevin, born in 1962, lives in Moscow, and has established a reputation as one of the most brilliant young Russian authors. His works of fiction include the novel *Omom Ra*, the novella *The Yellow Arrow*, and the story collections *The Blue Lantern* (winner of the Russian "Little Booker" Prize in 1993) and *A Werewolf Problem in Central Russia*.

VICTOR

PELEVIN

TRANSLATED FROM THE RUSSIAN

BY ANDREW BROMFIELD

THE LIFE

OF INSECTS

PENGUIN BOOKS

PENGUIN BOOKS

Published by the Penguin Group
Penguin Putnam Inc., 375 Hudson Street,
New York, New York 10014, U.S.A.
Penguin Books Ltd, 27 Wrights Lane,
London W8 5TZ, England
Penguin Books Australia Ltd, Ringwood,
Victoria, Australia
Penguin Books Canada Ltd, 10 Alcorn Avenue,
Toronto, Ontario, Canada M4V 3B2
Penguin Books (N.Z.) Ltd, 182–190 Wairau Road,
Auckland 10, New Zealand

Penguin Books Ltd, Registered Offices:
Harmondsworth, Middlesex, England

First published in Great Britain by Harbord Publishing 1996
First published in the United States of America
by Farrar, Straus and Giroux 1998
Published in Penguin Books 1999

1 3 5 7 9 10 8 6 4 2

Originally published in Russian in 1994 in *Znamya*, Moscow; published
in 1995 by Vagrius Publishing House, Moscow, as *Zhizn Nasekomyk*.

Epigraph from "Letters to a Roman Friend," by Joseph Brodsky,
translated by George L. Kline and published in *A Part of Speech*
(Farrar, Straus and Giroux, 1980)

THE LIBRARY OF CONGRESS HAS CATALOGUED THE
FARRAR STRAUS GIROUX EDITION AS FOLLOWS
Pelevin, Viktor.
[Zhizn´ nasekomykh. English]
The life of insects: a novel / Victor Pelevin; translated
from the Russian by Andrew Bromfield.
p. cm.
ISBN 0-374-18625-1 (hc.)
ISBN 0 14 02.7972 5 (pbk.)
I. Bromfield, Andrew.   II. Title.
PG3485.E38Z361.   1998
891.73´44—dc21   97–11106

Printed in the United States of America
Set in Transitional

CONTENTS

TRANSLATOR'S

NOTE

Mitya and Dima are both diminutive forms

of the Russian name Dmitry.

In the garden where I sit a torch is burning.

I'm alone — no lady, servant, or acquaintance.

Not the humble of this world, nor yet its mighty—

Nothing but the buzzing of an insect chorus.

— JOSEPH BRODSKY

THE LIFE

OF INSECTS

THE RUSSIAN FOREST

The main building of the old resort hotel, half hidden from view behind a screen of old poplars and cypresses, was an oppressive, gray structure which seemed to have turned its back to the sea at the bidding of some crazed fairy-tale conjuror. The façade, with its columns, cracked stars, and sheaves of wheat bent eternally before a plaster wind, faced into a shallow courtyard where the smells of the kitchen, the laundry, and the hairdresser's mingled; the massive wall which faced onto the shoreline had only two or three windows. A few yards from the colonnade there was a high concrete wall, beyond which the rays of the sunset glinted on the smokestacks of the local power plant. The tall formal doors concealed in the shade on the cyclopean balcony had been locked for so long that even the crack between them had disappeared under several layers of caked paint, and the yard was usually empty, except when an occasional truck cautiously squeezed its way in, bringing milk and bread from Feodosia.

This evening there wasn't even a truck in the yard, so there was no one to notice the individual leaning on the molded balustrade of the balcony, except perhaps for a pair of seagulls out on patrol, two white specks drifting across the sky. The stranger was looking down and to the right, toward the shelter on the dock and the cone of a loudspeaker lodged under the edge of its roof. The sea was noisy, but when the wind blew toward the hotel, it carried audible snatches of a radio broadcast directed at the deserted beach.

". . . not at all the same as each other, not cut to the same pattern . . . created us all different; is not this part of the grand scheme of things, counted, unlike the transient plans of man, in many . . . What does the Lord expect of us, as He turns His hopeful gaze in our direction? Will we be able to make use of His gift? . . . For He Himself does not know what to expect from the souls that He has sent to . . ."

Then came the strains of a church organ. The melody was majestic, but from time to time it was interrupted by an absurd "oompah-oompah"; in any case, there was no chance to become caught up in the music, because very quickly it was replaced once again by the voice of the announcer.

"You have been listening to a broadcast from a series especially prepared for our station by the American charity The Rivers of Babylon . . . on Sundays . . . to the following address: The Voice of God, Bliss, Idaho, U.S.A."

The loudspeaker fell silent, and the stranger crooked his index finger.

"Aha," he murmured, "it's Sunday today. That means there'll be dancing."

His appearance was unusual. Despite the warm evening, he was dressed in a gray three-piece suit, a cap, and a tie— the small southern-style Lenin statue standing below, entangled in grapevines all the way up to his silvery bosom, was dressed in almost identical fashion. But the figure gave no obvious sign of suffering from the heat and seemed entirely at ease, except for occasionally glancing at his watch, looking around, and whispering to himself.

The loudspeaker hissed senselessly for a few minutes and

then began intoning again in dreamy Ukrainian. At this point the man heard footsteps behind him and turned. Two people were walking toward him along the balcony: the first a short fat individual in white shorts and a brightly colored T-shirt, and behind him a foreigner in a panama hat, light shirt, and beige trousers, carrying a large briefcase. He was obviously a foreigner, recognizable as such not so much from the way he was dressed as from his fragile eyeglasses with thin black frames and the special tender tan of his skin, a subtle shade only acquired on shores far distant from the Crimea.

The individual in the cap pointed to his watch and waved his fist at the fat newcomer, who shouted back at him: "It's fast! It's always wrong."

They moved closer and embraced.

"Hi, Arnold," said the individual in the cap.

"Hello, Arthur. Let me introduce you," the fat newcomer said, turning to the foreigner. "This is Arthur, I told you about him. And this is Samuel Sacker. He speaks Russian."

"Just call me Sam," said the foreigner, extending his hand.

"Pleased to meet you," said Arthur. "How was your journey, Sam?"

"Just fine, thank you," replied Sam. "How are things here?"

"The same as ever," said Arthur. "You know how things are in Moscow, don't you, Sam? Well, it's basically the same here, only a bit more hemoglobin and glucose. And vitamins, too—the food's good here, lots of fruit and grapes."

"And then," added Arnold, "from what we hear, in the West you're choking to death on all kinds of repellents and insecticides, but our packaging is entirely pollution-free."

"But is it hygienic?"

"Pardon?"

"Is it hygienic? You mean skin, don't you?" said Sam.

Arnold was clearly a little embarrassed.

"Well now," said Arthur, breaking the awkward pause. "Will you be with us for long?"

"About three or four days, I think," said Sam.

"Will that be long enough for you to do your market research?"

"I wouldn't really call it research. I just want to gather a few impressions, get some general idea of whether it would be worth expanding our business here."

"Great," said Arthur. "I've already lined up a few typical specimens, I think first thing tomorrow morning . . ."

"Oh, no," said Sam, "no special Potemkin villages. I prefer to move around at random—strangely enough, that's the way you get the most accurate impression of the real situation. And not tomorrow morning, we'll start right now!"

"What?" gasped Arthur. "But what about a rest? Or a drink after the journey?"

"That's right," said Arnold. "Tomorrow would be better. And the places we choose. Otherwise, you'll get a distorted impression."

"If I do get a distorted impression, no doubt you'll have plenty of time to correct it," said Sam laconically.

With a confident athletic movement he leaped up to the balustrade of the balcony and sat there with his legs dangling in space. Instead of holding him back, the other two clambered onto the balustrade beside him. Arthur completed the maneuver with no difficulty, but Arnold managed it only on his second attempt, and unlike the other two he sat with his back to the yard, as though he was afraid the height might make him dizzy.

"Let's go," said Sam, and jumped down.

Arthur followed him without a word. Arnold sighed and tumbled backward after them, like a scuba diver throwing himself into the sea from the side of a boat.

•

If there had been a witness to this scene, we must assume he would have leaned over the balustrade, expecting to see three broken bodies lying on the ground below. But he would have seen nothing down there except eight small puddles, a crushed cigarette pack, and the cracks in the pavement.

On the other hand, if he possessed preternaturally sharp vision, he might just have discerned three mosquitoes in the distance, flying away in the direction of the village concealed behind the trees.

What would this imaginary observer have felt, what would he have done? Set off in confusion down the rusty fire escape which offered the only exit from the terrace that had been closed off for so long? Or would he—who knows?—have felt a new and unfamiliar sensation stirring in his soul and sat on the gray molded balustrade and tumbled after the threesome? I don't know. And probably no one knows what might be expected from someone who does not really exist yet possesses preternaturally sharp vision.

Sam looked around at his partners. Arthur and Arnold had turned into small mosquitoes of that miserable hue of gray familiar from prerevolutionary village huts, a color that in its time had reduced many a Russian poet to tears; they were staring in dull envy at their flying companion as he swayed in the current of warm air rising from the ground.

Only the inconvenient arrangement of his mouth organs prevented Sam Sacker from grinning complacently. He looked quite different from the others: he was a light chocolate color, with long elegant legs, a small tight belly, and wings swept back like a jet plane's. The transformed faces of Arthur and Arnold terminated in thick dowels resembling the needle of a titanic syringe or the speed gauge on the nose of a jet fighter, but Sam's lips extended elegantly into six fine, elastic appendices, with a long, pointed proboscis protruding from among them. In short, the American mosquito cut a fine figure alongside the two simple Russian insects. In addition, Arthur and Arnold flew with a womanish kind of breaststroke, while the way Sam's wings moved was more like a butterfly's, so he flew much faster and sometimes had to hover in the air to wait for his companions to catch up with him.

They flew in silence, Sam making wide circles around Arthur and Arnold, who watched his maneuvers sullenly. Arnold felt particularly bad, because the drop of ruby-red blood gleaming in his belly was dragging him down toward the ground. They couldn't tell where Sam was headed either, as he chose his route from signs that only he recognized, changing direction and height; at one point, for no obvious reason, he flew into a window, through a long empty attic, and out the far end. Eventually, a white wall with a blue-framed window appeared in front of them and they were enveloped in the dense shade of pear trees which grew around the house. Sam flew down toward a low window covered with white netting and landed on a board nailed crookedly in place to serve as a window ledge. Arnold and Arthur landed beside him. With the high-pitched buzzing of their wings no longer drowning out every other sound, they heard someone snoring behind the netting.

Sam looked inquiringly at Arthur.

"There should be a hole here in the corner," said Arthur. "Our colleagues usually make one."

The hole was a narrow gap between the frame and the netting. Arthur and Sam squeezed through it without particular difficulty, but Arnold had problems with his belly. He puffed and panted for some time, and got through only when his companions pulled him in after them.

It was dark inside, and the room smelled of eau de cologne, mold, and sweat. In the center of the room stood a large table covered with oilcloth. Beside it was a bed and a bedside table with a neat row of small, faceted eau-de-cologne bottles. Lying on the bed in a tangled pile of sheets was a seminaked body, with one blue track-suited leg dangling down to the floor. It was shuddering spasmodically in uneasy sleep and of course did not notice the appearance of three mosquitoes on the table not far from its head.

"What's that tattoo he has?" Sam asked softly, when his eyes had adjusted to the semidarkness. "I get the point of Lenin and Stalin, but why's he got OKWIFIP written underneath? Is it a name?"

"No," said Arthur, "it's an abbreviation. Our Kids Will Fix the Pigs."

"He hates pigs?"

"Well now," Arnold explained condescendingly, "it's a very complex cultural nexus. If I start explaining it now, we'll just get bogged down, quite literally. Let's get on with taking the sample now that we're here, while the subject is still asleep."

"Yes, yes," said Sam, "absolutely."

He soared up, performed a magnificent loop-the-loop above the sleeping figure, and landed on the stretch of thin, tender skin by the ear.

"Arnold," Arthur whispered admiringly, "look at that . . . He flies without making a sound."

"That's America for you," said Arnold. "You fly up and keep an eye on him, you never know what might happen."

"What about you?"

"I'll wait here," said Arnold, slapping a leg against the ruby drop in his belly.

Arthur took off and flew over to Sam, trying to buzz as little as possible. Sam still hadn't made a hole in the skin and was sitting there on its small hummocks, between which hairs grew up like young birch trees.

Sam stood up, leaned against one of the hairs, and fixed a thoughtful gaze on the distant hills of the nipples covered with thick reddish undergrowth.

"You know," he said, when Arthur landed beside him, "I do a lot of traveling, and what always astonishes me is the absolute uniqueness of every landscape. Not long ago I was in Mexico, and there's just no comparison. The natural world there's so rich, you know, too rich even. Sometimes you have to spend ages wandering through the pectoral chaparral before you find a good place to drink your fill. And you can't let your guard down for a moment, or a wild louse might fall on you from the hair tops, and then . . ."

"You mean a louse can attack you?" Arthur asked skeptically.

"Well, you see, Mexican lice are very lazy, and of course it's easier for them to suck blood from the delicate belly of a mosquito than to earn their food through honest work. They're very clumsy, though, and you usually have time to fly off if one attacks. But in the air you might get brought down by a flea. It's a very hard world, a cruel world, but very beautiful at the same time. I must admit I prefer Japan. You know, those long open expanses of yellow with almost no vegetation, but still not like a desert. When you look down on them from above, it feels like you've gone back to some really ancient time. But you have to see it all for yourself, of course. There's nothing more beautiful than a pair of Japanese buttocks gently gilded by the first ray of dawn, with a delicate breeze blowing . . . God, how beautiful life can be!"

"And do you like it here?"

"Every landscape has its charms," Sam replied evasively. "I'd compare this place," he said, nodding in the direction of the ear drooping down over the neck below him, "with Canada near the Great Lakes. But everything here is closer to a wild state, all the smells are natural . . ." He prodded the base of a hair with one leg. "We've forgotten what the great mother skin actually smells like . . ."

From the intonation Sam used for these last few words, Arthur realized he was showing off his knowledge of Russian slang.

"In general," added Sam, "it's the same difference as between Japan and China."

"Have you been to China, too?" asked Arthur.

"A couple of times."

"And Africa?"

"Lots of times."

"How was it?"

"I can't say I liked it very much. It's like being on another planet. Everything's black and murky. And then, don't get me wrong, I'm no racist, but the local mosquitoes . . ."

Arthur couldn't think of anything else to ask, and Sam set to work with a polite smile. The way he went about it was unusual. He bent back his side appendices, then his sharp proboscis started vibrating with incredible speed, finally sinking into the ground at the foot of the nearest hair like a knife cutting through salami.

Arthur was also intending to drink his fill, but when he thought of the crunching sound his crude, thick nose would make breaking through the stubborn surface of the skin, he felt ashamed and decided to wait awhile. Sam managed to hit a capillary at his first attempt, and his brown belly gradually began turning a reddish color.

The surface beneath their feet quaked, and there was a low mumbling exhalation. Arthur was sure the body was doing this for its own internal reasons, unconnected with what was happening, but he still felt a little anxious.

"Sam," he said, "finish up now. This isn't your Japan."

Sam paid absolutely no attention to him. Arthur looked at him and shuddered. Sam's downy face, which only a minute ago had been filled with cultured intelligence, was now strangely distorted, and the hairy convex eyes, circled by thin black lines that looked like wire-rim glasses, no longer expressed anything at all, as though the mirror of the soul had been transformed into two burned-out headlights. Arthur went over and nudged Sam gently.

"Hey," he said insistently, "time to go."

Sam didn't react at all. Arthur nudged him harder, but he seemed to be rooted to the ground, while his belly kept swelling. Suddenly the body under their feet began to turn and gave out a hoarse growl. Arthur leaped up in panic.

"Arnold! Come here!" he shouted as loud as he could. But Arnold, alarmed by the fuss and the shouting, was already there.

"Why are you buzzing fit to wake the whole room?"

"Something's wrong with Sam," said Arthur. "I think he's paralyzed. I can't shake him out of it."

"Let's take him by the wings. Aha, that's it. Careful, you're stepping on his foot. Sam, can you fly?"

Sam nodded weakly. The skin he was standing on trembled and began leaning to the right.

"Into the air, quickly! He's getting up! Sam, flap your wings, or it'll be too late!" Arthur shouted, supporting Sam's swollen trunk and avoiding his wings, which were waving senselessly back and forth.

Somehow they managed to make a landing on the bedside table. The body rose from the bed, loomed over the mosquitoes, and in terrible silence the black shadow of a huge open palm hurtled toward them from the ceiling. Just as Arthur and Arnold were preparing to abandon Sam to his fate and shoot off in opposite directions, the palm changed direction, neatly grasped one of the bottles standing on the small table, and retreated upward. There was a distant creaking of springs, as the body staggered back to the bed.

"Arthur," Arnold asked softly, "do you know what's in those bottles?"

"It's our forest," Sam suddenly spoke. "Our Russian forest."

"What forest?"

"Cypress sweetness," Sam replied incomprehensibly.

"Sam, are you all right?" asked Arnold.

"Me?" Sam chuckled ominously. "Sure I am. And we're gonna sort you out, too, believe it!"

"Let's get him into the fresh air quick," Arthur said anxiously.

Arnold nodded and tried to lift Sam up, but Sam suddenly slapped him in the face with his wing, soared into the air, and raced over to the window. Slipping with incredible deftness through the narrow gap between the window frame and the netting, he flew out into the blue southern sky, which was already thickening into dusk.

•

The next morning was quiet. The fog descending from the mountains flowed into the avenues lined with cypresses, so that from high above it looked as though the surface, bisected by green dams, hid bottomless depths—or, if there was a bottom to them, it was very deep. The rare passersby somehow seemed like fish swimming slowly, close to the surface. Their forms were blurred, and Arthur and Arnold had already flown down twice in vain, mistaking first a soaking-wet cardboard box a television had come in, and then a small haystack covered with plastic sheeting, for Sam Sacker.

"Maybe he got a lift to Feodosia," said Arthur, breaking the silence.

"Maybe," said Arnold. "Maybe anything at all."

"Look," said Arthur, "isn't that him?"

"No," said Arnold, looking closely, "it's not him. It's a statue of a volleyball player."

"No, over there, by that kiosk. Coming out of the bushes."

Arnold saw a large object that looked from a distance like a huge ball of dung. The object tumbled out of the bushes, wobbling as it rolled over to the bench and plonked itself down, stretching out oddly thin legs in front of itself.

"Let's land," said Arnold.

A minute later they emerged from behind the empty newspaper kiosk, examined the ten or fifteen feet of space to which their vision was limited, and then sat down on the bench beside the fat man. There was no doubt it was Sam, but a very different Sam from the one who had stood on the balcony of the hotel the evening before. It wasn't his swollen belly—that transformation, perfectly normal for mosquitoes, didn't warrant any special attention; it was the face, which was the same but seemed to be stuffed full of something, with a heaviness reminiscent not so much of a goose stuffed with apples as an apple stuffed with a goose.

"Damn," thought Arthur, as he looked at the foreigner's terrifyingly calm profile, "perhaps he shouldn't take that blood group? Perhaps he has an allergy?"

"You were hard to find, Sam," said Arnold.

"Who needs to look?" said Sam. "Here I am, right here. Got here all by myself."

He spoke in a new, unfamiliar voice, thick and slow.

"Where did you spend the night?" Arthur asked. "Surely not here on the bench? You're a stranger here, and some of the types around . . ."

Sam suddenly turned to face Arthur and grabbed him by the lapels.

"Stop that, Sam," growled Arthur, trying to pull his hands away. "Let go! Let go! People are looking!"

It wasn't true. Nobody was watching them except for a confused Arnold.

"Own up, you bastard," Sam said sternly. "You suck Russian blood, don't you?"

"Yes," Arthur replied softly.

Sam freed one hand and gripped Arnold's neck with fingers of iron.

"And so do you?"

"Yes, I do."

The hand pressed on Arnold's shoulders with such force that he sank down under it like a weightlifter trying to raise a weight too heavy for him; he even recalled the heavy statue hand of stone from some now forgotten tragedy which he had read when he was still a larva. Sam sank into silence, as though pondering what to say next.

"So why do you suck Russian blood?" he asked stupidly, about three minutes later.

"We get thirsty," Arthur replied plaintively. Arnold couldn't see him; his view was blocked by Sam's protruding belly, which billowed like some lonely red sail in the sunset. Arnold felt insulted by the humiliation in his colleague's voice.

"What are you getting at, anyway?" he asked caustically. "We suck everybody's blood. Don't you do the same? Anyone who talks like that just wants to keep it all, down to the very last drop, for himself. Look at that belly. Arthur and I wouldn't drink that much in a week."

Sam let go of Arthur and set his palm against the huge quivering paunch.

"Arise, O vast and mighty land," he mumbled and struggled to his feet, almost smearing Arnold across the bench with his hand. He threw his head back and took several quick gulps of air, then hung his head forward, but instead of sneezing as this gesture might suggest, he flooded the asphalt in front of him with a stream of dark cherry-colored vomit smelling of blood and eau de cologne, and his huge belly immediately shrank to half its size.

"Where am I?" he asked, looking around, his voice sounding a little more like the old Sam's.

"There's nothing to be afraid of," said the half-crushed Arnold, feeling the hand on his shoulder relaxing its pressure.

Sam shook his head and looked down at the huge bloody puddle at his feet.

"What's going on?" he asked again.

"There's been a technical error," said Arthur. "You got a damaged specimen. Please don't think that everyone here drinks Russian Forest cologne . . ."

At these words Sam's eyes clouded over again, and he renewed his grip on Arthur and Arnold.

"Come on," he said.

"Where to?" asked Arthur, frightened.

"You'll see. So the bastards got thirsty, did they . . ."

•

Dragging his struggling companions after him, Sam took several massive strides along the lane toward the boardwalk, and then he puked again, making a more thorough job of it this time. Arthur and Arnold were splashed and scalded by the incredibly smelly dark, wide stream as it flooded down the pavement. Now Arnold felt the same fingers that had been dragging him along like the hook on a tractor clutching at his neck for support.

"I think that's all of it," he said to Arthur, grabbing hold of Sam's arm. "Let's take him down to the boardwalk, so he can get a breath of air."

"What was wrong with him?" asked Arthur.

"Psychologically unstable. Drank too much of that eau-de-cologne cocktail and lost control. Went into a sort of trance."

The lane came to an end, and the three of them set off along the boardwalk. Sam was already walking by himself, swaying slightly and adjusting his glasses, one of the lenses of which was newly cracked.

"Sam, are you all right?" said Arnold.

"I think so," Sam answered in a weak voice.

"Can you walk on your own?"

"Gentlemen," said Sam, "please accept my apologies. I am horrified at my behavior."

"Nonsense," Arnold said cheerfully. "Don't even think about it. It's already forgotten."

"I told you," said Arthur, "that you should have had a rest first."

"I apologize," said Sam. "But where's my briefcase?"

Arnold looked around. The briefcase was nowhere to be seen.

"That's bad luck. What did you have in it? Anything valuable?"

"Nothing special. Material for preserving samples, a camcorder. But how can I take any samples now?"

"It's obvious you must have left it back there," said Arnold. "We'll go straight back . . . All right, all right, Sam. I understand. I'll fly back there myself and check things out."

"What an emotional whirlwind!" said Sam. "What a torrent of feeling! I was almost overwhelmed, believe me."

Arthur and Arnold cautiously seated the thin, trembling figure on the bench and sat down themselves on either side of it. Sam was still shaking.

"Calm down, Sam," Arnold whispered in a motherly voice. "Look how calm and peaceful everything is here. Look at the seagulls flying and the girls walking by. There's a boat sailing past. Beautiful, isn't it?"

Sam raised his eyes. The first tourists were wandering along the jetty through the fog. From the direction of the seaside café he could hear two voices: a child's voice asking something unintelligible, and an authoritative bass, which gave an equally unintelligible answer.

Out of the fog appeared a short man with a mustache, wearing a track suit. Behind him plodded a boy carrying a plastic beach bag with something heavy inside. He caught up with the man and began walking beside him, glancing sideways at Sam and his companions. The boy was wearing blue flip-flops, and he was dragging his left foot, because one of the rubber straps was broken.

2

INITIATION

"Pa, did you see how strange those men were?" the boy said when the kiosk was behind them.

His father spat on the road. "Drunks," he said. "If you behave like that, you'll grow up like them, too."

A piece of caked dung had appeared in his hands. He tossed it to his son, and the boy barely managed to stretch out his hands in time. He couldn't understand from what his father had said just how he should or shouldn't behave so as to grow up like the strange men, but as soon as the warm dung slapped against his palms, everything seemed clear, and the boy dropped his father's present into his plastic bag without saying a word.

A long narrow pavilion loomed out of the fog, looking like a box of matches standing on end. Inside it, behind the motley packs of cigarettes, the bottles of scent, and a long display of smoked sausage sticks and vibrators, sat a bored saleswoman. Smoke was rising from the filthy glass door of an electric grill behind her, in which indifferent rows of white chicken were roasting. A loudspeaker hung on the wall of the pavilion, and music emerged from it in bursts, as though it was being forced out through the plastic grid by an invisible bicycle pump.

"Excuse me, which way is it to the beach?" the father asked the saleswoman.

She stuck her hand out through the small window and pointed silently into the mist.

"Hmm . . . And how much are those small glasses?" the father asked.

The woman answered him in a soft voice.

"That much!" said the father. "Okay, I'll take them."

He handed the glasses to his son, who put them into his bag, and they went on. The pavilion disappeared from view, and a small bridge appeared in front of them. Beyond it, the fog was even thicker; the only thing they could see was the concrete beneath their feet. Off to the sides, blurred strips of green drifted past them, looking like huge blades of grass, or perhaps trees. Instead of the sky over their heads, there was a low white vault of fog, and on their left they occasionally saw empty stone planters with ribbed sides, which widened toward the tops, so they resembled corks from bottles of wine turned upside down.

"Pa," asked the boy, "what's fog made of?"

His father thought for a moment.

"Fog," he said, holding out several small clumps of dung to his son, "is extremely fine droplets of water hanging in the air."

"Then why don't they fall down?"

His father pondered and held out another clump to his son.

"Because they are very small," he said.

Once again, the boy didn't see where his father was getting the dung from, and he glanced around him as though trying to make out the tiny droplets.

"We won't get lost, will we?" he asked anxiously. "It doesn't look as though there's going to be any beach."

His father didn't answer. He walked on through the fog

without speaking, and there was nothing for the boy to do but follow. The boy felt as though he and his father were crawling along at the foot of the biggest Christmas tree in the world, moving through immense mounds of cotton wool meant to look like snow, not really knowing where they were going, and his father was only pretending to know the way.

"Pa, where are we going? We just keep walking and walking . . ."

"What?"

"I just . . ."

The boy looked up and saw a dim glimmer off to one side. In the murk he couldn't see where it was coming from, or what it was that was shining. Perhaps it was part of the fog gleaming with a blue light right beside him, or perhaps the beam of a searchlight switched on by some distant hand was trying to pierce the fog.

"Pa, look!"

His father looked up and stopped.

"What is it?"

"I don't know," said his father, walking on. "They probably forgot to switch off one of the streetlamps."

The boy set off after him, his eyes following the light as it drifted away from them.

They walked in silence for several more minutes. The boy looked around now and then, but he couldn't see the light anymore. Strange thoughts unlike any he'd had before began filling his mind, thoughts he would never have had in an ordinary place.

"Pa, listen," said the boy. "I feel like we got lost ages ago and we only think we're going to the beach but there isn't any beach at all. It even makes me feel afraid . . ."

His father laughed and tousled the boy's hair. Then suddenly he was holding a huge piece of dung, big enough to make the head of a dung man.

"You know what they say," he said. "Life is no bed of roses."

The boy nodded slyly and squeezed his father's present into the bag with difficulty, shifting his grip on the handles because the thin plastic sheet was beginning to stretch.

"You shouldn't be afraid," said his father. "There's no need . . . You're a man, after all, a soldier. Here."

The boy took the new piece of dung and tried to hold on to it, but he dropped it right away, and then the plastic bag fell on the concrete too, the glasses crunching as they broke. The boy squatted down by the bag, from which a lot of the dung had spilled out: he touched a piece, then raised his frightened eyes to his father, but instead of the grim frown he was expecting he saw an expression of solemn and somehow official tenderness.

"Now you're a grown man," his father said after a pause, and held out another handful of dung to his son. "Think of today as your second birthday."

"Why?"

"From now on, you won't be able to carry all your dung. From now on, you'll have your own Ai, just like me and your mother."

"My own Ai?" asked the boy. "But what's an Ai?"

"See for yourself."

The boy peered at his father and saw beside him a large, semitransparent blue-brown sphere.

"What's that?" he asked, frightened.

"That's my Ai," said his father. "And now you'll have one just like it."

"But why didn't I see it before?"

"You were too young. But now you're old enough to see the sacred sphere for yourself."

"But why does it flicker and fade like that? What's it made of?"

"You think it's flickering because you're seeing it for the first time. When you get used to it, you'll understand it's more real than anything else in the world. And it's made of pure dung."

"Aah," said the boy slowly, "so that's where you were getting all the dung from. You just kept on giving it to me, and I couldn't tell where you were getting it from. But now it turns out you've got all that. What was that word you said?"

"Ai. It's a sacred Egyptian syllable that dung beetles have used for thousands of years as the name for their spheres," his father said solemnly. "Your Ai is still small, but it will gradually get bigger and bigger. Your mother and I will give you some of the dung, and then you'll learn to find it for yourself."

The boy was still squatting there, looking up at his father doubtfully. His father smiled and smacked his lips.

"But where will I find the dung?" the boy asked.

"All around," said his father, and gestured into the fog with his hand.

"But there isn't any dung there, Pa."

"On the contrary, there's nothing but dung."

"I don't understand," said the boy.

"Hold this. Now you'll be able to understand. Everything around you becomes dung once you have an Ai. And then you'll have the whole world in your hands. And you'll push it along in front of you."

"How can I push the whole world along in front of me?"

His father put his hand on the sphere and shoved it forward slightly.

"This is the whole world," he said.

"I still don't understand," said the boy. "How can this ball of dung be the whole world? How can the whole world be a ball of dung?"

"Take your time," said his father. "Wait until your Ai is bigger. Then you'll understand."

"That ball's not very big."

"It just seems that way," said his father. "Look how much dung I've given you today. But my Ai hasn't got any smaller."

"But if it's the whole world, then what is everything else?"

"What everything else?"

"Just everything else."

His father smiled patiently. "I know it's difficult to understand, but there simply isn't anything other than dung. Everything I see around me," he said, making a wide gesture through the fog, "is really only Ai. And the purpose of life is to push it along in front of you. Do you understand me? When you look around you, all you see is the Ai from the inside."

The boy frowned and thought for a minute. Then with his hands he began scraping together the dung that had tumbled out in front of him, and in a few minutes with remarkable ease he had shaped a sphere—not a very smooth and round one, but still unmistakably a sphere. The sphere was precisely the same height as the boy, and he thought that was odd.

"Pa," he said, "all the dung I had just now was one bagful, but this is half a truckload. Where did it come from?"

"That's all the dung your mother and I have given you since you were born," said his father. "You were carrying it with you all the time, only you couldn't see it."

The boy examined the sphere poised in front of him.

"So now I have to push it along?"

His father nodded.

"And everything around me is just this ball?"

His father nodded again.

"But how can I see this ball from the inside and push it along at the same time?"

"I don't know that myself." His father shrugged. "When you grow up, you can become a philosopher and explain it to the rest of us."

"All right," said the boy, "if there isn't anything except dung, then who am I? I'm not made of dung, am I?"

"I'll try to explain," said his father, pushing his hands into his sphere and passing one more handful to his son. "That's right, that's the way, with open hands . . . Now take a close look at your own sphere. It is you."

"That can't be right! I'm here," said the boy, pointing to himself with his thumb.

"You're thinking about it the wrong way. Try logical reasoning. If you call something Ai, then it means it's you. Your Ai is you."

"My you is Ai?" asked the boy. "Or your you?"

"No," said his father. "Your Ai is you. Sit on this bench here and take it easy, and then you'll see it all for yourself."

What the father called a bench was a long, thick beam with a square cross section, lying at the edge of their limited field of vision. One end of it had been badly burned—it had obviously been caught by the flames from a garbage can someone had set on fire—and now the bench looked like a match enlarged many times over. The boy rolled his Ai over to the bench, sat down, and looked at his father.

"Won't the fog make it hard to see?" he asked.

"No," said his father. "Look, you can almost see your Ai now. Only don't look anywhere else."

The boy looked at his father, shrugged skeptically, and stared at the uneven surface of his freshly molded sphere. As he gazed at it, it gradually became smoother, and even began to gleam. Then it started to turn transparent, and inside it he could see something moving. The boy shuddered.

From deep inside the sphere he was being watched by a spiky black head with tiny eyes and powerful jaws. The creature had no neck; its head was connected directly to a hard black shell, with two rows of serrated black legs wriggling along its edges.

"What's that?" the boy asked.

"It's a reflection."

"Of what?"

"What a question! I thought you understood everything. Let's try logic again. You ask yourself: If I see a reflection in front of me and I know that in front of me is my Ai, what is it that I'm seeing?"

"Myself, probably," said the boy.

"There you are," said his father. "Now you've got it."

The boy began to think it over.

"But a reflection is always in something," he said, raising

his eyes to his father's black horned face with the gleaming beady eyes.

"That's right," said his father. "But what of it?"

"What is the reflection in?"

"What do you mean? You're really making a mountain out of this. It's all there in front of your eyes. It's in itself, where else could it be?"

The boy said nothing for a long time as he gazed into the sphere of dung, and then he covered his face with his front legs.

"Yes," he said finally, in a changed voice. "Of course. Ai understand. This is Ai. Of course it is."

"Well done," said his father, scrambling down from the match and rising up slightly on his back four legs in order to grab hold of his sphere with the front two. "Let's get moving."

•

The mist around them had become so dense that it resembled the clouds of steam in a bathhouse, and they could judge how fast they were moving only by the cracks in the pavement, which slowly drifted past and away behind them. Every ten feet or so, the gaps between the paving slabs, caked with dirt, some with grass growing in them, emerged from the whiteness of oblivion. At the edges of the slabs there were shallow grooves with rusty iron staples meant for the hook of a crane. They could see nothing else of the outside world.

"Do only dung beetles have Ais?" the boy asked.

"Oh, no. All insects have Ais. In fact, all insects really are their Ais. But only scarabs are able to see them. And the scarabs know that the whole world is also part of their Ai— that's why they say they push the world along in front of them."

"Then does that mean that everyone else is a dung beetle too, if they all have Ais?"

"Of course. But the dung beetles who know about it are called scarabs. The scarabs are the ones who possess the ancient knowledge of the essential meaning of life," said his father, slapping one leg against his sphere.

"Are you a scarab, Pa?"

"Yes."

"And am I?"

"Not quite yet," said his father. "You still have to experience the fundamental mystery."

"But what is the fundamental mystery?"

"Well now, my son," said the father, "its nature is so far beyond comprehension that it's best not even to talk about it. You just wait until it happens."

"Will I have to wait long?"

"I don't know," said his father. "Maybe a minute, maybe three years."

He breathed out as he pushed his sphere farther on, and then ran after it.

The boy watched his father and painstakingly copied every movement he made. Every time his father pushed his sphere, hands sank deep into the dung, and the boy couldn't understand how he managed to pull them out again quickly enough.

The boy tried to thrust his own hands as deeply into his own sphere, and at the third attempt he succeeded; all he had to do was to squeeze his fingers together first. At it turned, the sphere dragged his hands around with it, and they jerked free only when it seemed his feet were about to be lifted from the ground. "What if I push them even deeper?" the boy thought, and he thrust his hands into the sphere as hard as he could. The sphere rolled forward, the boy's feet rose from the ground, and his heart skipped a beat, as if he were going over the top on a swing for the first time. He flew upward, halted motionless for a moment at the highest point of noon, and was hurled downward by the motion of the sphere rolling across the concrete. As he fell, he realized that the sphere would roll over him, but there was no time to feel frightened. Darkness fell, and when the boy came to his senses, he was being hoisted up by the same hemisphere of dung that had just flattened him against the pavement.

"Good morning!" he heard his father's voice say. "How did you sleep?"

"What's happening, Pa?" the boy asked, fighting his dizziness.

"It's just life, son," said his father.

Glancing to one side, the boy saw a gray-brown sphere rolling through the murk. His father was nowhere to be seen, but when he looked closer, the boy could make out a blurred, indistinct silhouette on the surface of the dung, rotating with the movement of the sphere. The silhouette had a vague trunk, arms, legs, and even two eyes, which were gazing simultaneously into the sphere and out from it. The eyes looked at the boy sadly.

"Don't say it, son, don't say it. Ai know what you're going to ask. Yes. This happens to everyone. It's just that we scarabs are the only ones who can see it."

"Pa," asked the little sphere, "why did Ai used to think that you were walking behind your ball of dung and pushing it along?"

"That was because you were still a little boy, son."

"And is all of life like this, smashing your face against the concrete . . ."

"But life is fine and beautiful, anyway," said his father in a slightly threatening tone. "Good night."

The boy glanced ahead and saw the concrete slab advancing toward his eyes.

"Good morning!" said the big sphere when the darkness was dissipated once again. "How are you feeling?"

"Not good," the boy answered.

"Well, try harder to feel good. You're young and healthy —what have you got to feel sad about? Either . . ."

The big sphere shuddered and fell silent.

"Don't you hear anything?" it asked the little sphere.

"No," said the little sphere. "What should Ai hear?"

"It sounded like . . . No, Ai imagined it," said the big sphere. "What was Ai talking about?"

"About feeling good."

"Yes. After all, we're responsible for our own mood and everything else, too. We have to make an effort, in order . . . There it is again."

"What?" asked the little sphere.

"Footsteps. Can't you hear them?"

"No. Where?"

"Ahead of us," answered the big sphere. "Like an elephant running along."

"You're imagining it," said the little sphere. "Good night!"

"Good night!"

"Good morning!"

"Good morning!" the big sphere said, sighing. "Maybe Ai am imagining it. You know, Ai'm getting old. My health plays tricks on me. Sometimes in the morning Ai wake up and Ai think Ai'll be rolling along somewhere and suddenly something will happen . . ."

"What do you mean?" said the small sphere. "You're not old at all."

"Yes, Ai am, Ai'm old," the big sphere answered sadly. "Soon you'll have to take care of me, but you probably won't want to . . ."

"What are you saying, of course Ai'll want to."

"That's what you think now. But you'll have your own life and . . . there it is again."

"There what is again?" the small sphere asked impatiently.

"Footsteps. Ah . . . now there's a bell chiming. Can't you hear it?"

The big sphere stopped.

"Let's roll on," said the small sphere.

"No," said the big sphere, "you roll on, and Ai'll catch up with you."

"All right," the little sphere agreed, and disappeared into the fog.

The big sphere remained where he had stopped. He

couldn't hear any more footsteps, and he slowly set off once again.

"Son!" he shouted. "Hey! Where are you?"

"Ai'm here," answered a voice from the fog. "Good night!"

"Good night!"

"Good morning!"

"Good morning!" shouted the big sphere, and set off after the answering voice, and he rolled quite a long time before he realized that he and his son had missed each other.

"Hey!" he shouted again. "Where are you?"

"Ai'm here."

This time the voice came from a long way off, to his left. The big sphere was just about to move in that direction, but he suddenly froze in fright. Ahead of him he heard a thunderous blow, so powerful that the concrete beneath him shuddered slightly. The next blow was closer, and the dung sphere saw a huge red shoe with a stiletto heel stabbing down into the concrete a few feet ahead.

"Pa! Now Ai can hear footsteps, too! What is it?" he heard his son ask from far away.

"Son!" the father cried out despairingly.

"Pa!"

The boy cried out in terror and looked up. He glimpsed a shadow over his head, and for a moment he thought he saw a red shoe with a dark spot on the sole rising up into the sky, and then he thought that up in those ineffable heights into which the shoe had vanished the silhouette of an immense bird with its wings spread had appeared. With a struggle, the boy freed his hands from the sphere of dung and rushed over to where he had last heard his father's voice. After a few steps he came across a large black spot on the pavement, and he slipped on it and almost fell.

"Pa," he said gently.

Seeing what was left of his father was too painful, and he wandered back to his sphere, gradually absorbing what had happened. He remembered his father's kind face with the chitinous horns that weren't nearly as fearsome as they looked, and the beady eyes filled with love, and he began to cry. Then he remembered how his pa would hold out a piece of dung and say that tears did nothing to ease grief, and he stopped crying.

"Pa's soul has flown up to heaven," he thought, remembering the dark spot being borne aloft so rapidly on the immense sole of the red shoe, "and there's nothing Ai can do to help him now."

He looked up at his sphere and was amazed to see how big it had grown. Then he looked at his hands and sighed as he placed them against the warm yielding surface of the dung. With a final glance toward the place where his father's life had been cut short—he could see nothing but the fog now—he pushed his Ai on.

The sphere was now so massive that it required his full attention and all his strength, and the boy became totally absorbed in his strenuous work. Vague thoughts flitted through his mind, first about fate, then about his pa, then about himself. Soon he got the hang of it, and all he had to do was run along after the sphere on his thin black legs, with his face raised slightly so that the long chitinous protrusion on his lower jaw wouldn't catch on the sphere. After another few steps, his front legs sank deeply enough into the sphere, and the sphere lifted him up, then smashed him down against the concrete, and life began to take its normal course, the one followed by the sphere as it rolled ever on.

The concrete slab rose to meet his eyes, and darkness fell, and when the light came back, he had only a feeble recollection of the dream that had seemed so good only a minute before.

"Ai'll grow up and get married, Ai'll have children, and Ai'll teach them everything my pa taught me. And Ai'll be as kind to them as my pa was with me, and when Ai get old, they'll take care of me, and we'll all live a long and happy life," he thought, as he woke up and rose with the smooth rounded surface to meet a new day of movement toward the beach through the cold fog.

3

VIVRE POUR VIVRE

Up above, there was only the sky, with the cloud at its center looking like a flat face smiling gently with its eyes closed. Down below, for a long time nothing could be seen but the fog, and when it finally cleared, Marina was so tired she could hardly keep herself up in the air. From high up, few signs of civilization were visible: a few massed concrete jetties, wooden sheds at the edge of a beach, the buildings of a resort hotel, and some small houses on the distant slopes. She could still see the huge dish of the antenna gazing up from the peak of the hill, and the trailer standing beside it. The antenna and the trailer were closer than anything else to the sky out of which Marina was slowly descending, and she could see the antenna was old and rusty, the door of the trailer was nailed shut with crisscrossed planks, and the glass in its windows was broken. It all seemed rather sad, but the wind carried her on past, and she immediately forgot everything she'd seen. Stretching out her semitransparent wings, she flew a circle of farewell, cast an upward glance into the infinite blueness above her head, and tried to choose a place to land.

There wasn't really very much of a choice. The only empty

space large enough was on the boardwalk, and Marina swooped down over the slabs of concrete, beginning to move her legs while she was still in the air. The landing almost ended in disaster because there were drainage grids set in the concrete, and it was a miracle Marina didn't catch her stiletto heel in one of them. When her legs touched the ground, she ran on quickly, her red heels thumping against the concrete until her momentum was spent, and then she stopped and looked around.

The first object she encountered in this new world was a large plywood board with pictures of the Soviet future that never was and of the fine, beautiful people who lived in it. Marina peered intently for a minute at their faded Slavic faces, above which space stations were suspended in infinity, and then she turned her attention to the poster which covered half the billboard. It was handwritten with a Magic Marker on cheap newsprint:

THE ALIENS AMONG US
A lecture on flying saucers and their pilots.
New facts. A display of photographs.
The lecture will be followed by
A SESSION OF HYPNOTIC HEALING
All welcome
The lecture and the session of hypnosis will be
conducted by the prize-winning member
of the Voronezh Psychics Congress,
A. U. Spiderov, Ph.D. Technical Science

The last wisps of fog trembled in the bushes behind the poster, but the sky overhead was clear and the sun was shining with all its might. At the end of the boardwalk there was an overpass across an open drain that emptied into the sea, and Marina could hear music coming from a kiosk beyond it, just the right kind of music for a sunny morning on the beach. To Marina's right, on a bench in front of the public showers, an old man with a thick mane of yellowish-gray hair was dozing, and a short distance to her left, beside a set of scales that looked like small gallows, a woman in a white nurse's coat waited for customers.

Marina heard a rustling of wings, and when she raised her head she saw two female ants descending, repeating the same maneuvers she had performed a few minutes earlier. They had bags exactly like Marina's hanging on their shoulders, and they were dressed exactly the same way, in denim skirts, blouses from coop workshops, and red shoes with stiletto heels. The one flying in front and slightly lower swooped over the boardwalk and hurtled out over the sea, regaining altitude as she went. The second was about to land, then obviously changed her mind and began flapping her wings rapidly in an attempt to ascend again, but it was too late and she crashed full tilt into the window of a kiosk. Marina heard a tinkling of broken glass and screams and looked away, noticing only that several passersby were dashing to the scene.

Another newly landed female came ambling along the boardwalk, stretching her wings up into the air and using her handbag to keep her balance. Marina adjusted the strap of her bag on her shoulder, swung around, and set off leisurely along a row of benches.

She had a light and peaceful feeling, and if only her shoes didn't pinch, everything would have been just fine. She met men in bathing trunks with tanned hairy bodies walking in the opposite direction. They ran their eyes appreciatively over Marina's trim figure, and every glance gave her a warm feeling and started a sweet churning in her stomach. Marina reached the span over the small stream, spent a moment admiring the white strip of foam along the boundary between sea and dry land, listened to the pebbles tumbling beneath the waves, and then turned back.

After she had gone a few steps, she felt a vague yearning —it was time to do something. Marina couldn't figure out what exactly, until she paid attention to the gentle sound behind her back. Then she remembered.

The wings that had been dragging along in the dust behind

her were no longer needed. She went to the edge of the pavement, glanced on both sides, and plunged into the bushes. There she squatted down, put her hand back over her shoulder, wrapped it tight around the base of one wing, and pulled as hard as she could. Nothing happened; the wing was too firmly attached. Marina pulled at the other one. No better. Then she wrinkled her forehead and set to thinking.

"Ah, that's right," she muttered and opened her handbag. The first thing her hand encountered was a small file.

It didn't hurt when she filed the wings off, but it wasn't a pleasant feeling. She was particularly irritated by the scraping sound, which gave her a feeling like a toothache in her shoulder blades. At last the wings fell off into the grass, and the only traces left of them were the protrusions beside her shoulder blades and the holes in her blouse. Marina shoved the file back into her handbag, and the feeling of joyful peace returned. She darted out of the bushes onto the light-drenched boardwalk.

The world around her was beautiful. But what exactly made it so beautiful was hard to say. The objects that furnished this world—the trees, the benches, the clouds, the passersby—none seemed to be special in any way, but together they offered a clear promise of happiness, promised for no apparent reason at all. Marina heard a question spoken within herself, not in words, but its meaning was obvious: "What do you want, Marina?"

Marina thought for a moment and gave a cunning answer, also not in words, but she put into it all the stubborn hope of her young organism.

"That's the way life is!" she whispered, drawing the air that smelled of the sea deep into her lungs, and she set off along the boardwalk to meet the bright day ahead. Just as she was thinking she ought to do something to amuse herself, she spotted an arrow nailed to a tree, with the words:

SIFLIT COOP
*Videobar with continuous showing
of French feature films*

The arrow pointed to a path leading to a gray building behind the trees, and Marina decided to follow it.

The videobar proved to be a musty basement with paint crudely slapped on the walls, empty cigarette packs on the bar, and a flickering screen in one corner. As soon as she stepped inside, Marina was stopped by a rotund man in a track suit who demanded an entrance fee of two rubles sixty kopecks. Marina groped in her handbag for a small purse made of black imitation leather. In the purse she found two crumpled one-ruble notes and three twenty-kopeck pieces. She tipped them into the muscular palm, which grasped the money with three fingers and pointed with a fourth to one of the tables.

Most of those around her were recently landed girls in blouses with holes in their backs. The television, which they were gazing at as though bewitched, looked very much like a large aquarium, with a rainbow-colored ripple occasionally running across its one transparent side. Marina made herself comfortable and also began watching the aquarium.

Swimming about in it was a fleshy-faced middle-aged man with a sheepskin coat thrown over his shoulders. He swam up to the glass, stared damply at Marina, and then got into a red car and went home. He lived in a big apartment with his wife and a young servant who looked like Joan of Arc, who according to the plot was apparently not supposed to be his lover, but the way she acted made Marina wonder whether he was in fact screwing her while the film was being made.

The man loved a lot of women. He would stand by a window streaming with rain while they put their arms around his shoulders and dreamily pressed one cheek against his strong reliable back. There was an obvious contradiction in the film here: Marina could see that the man's back was very reliable (in her imagination she even pressed her own cheek against it), but he always left his women weeping in hotel bedrooms on foggy mornings, and somehow this didn't affect the reliability of his back in the slightest. In order to flesh out the romantic side of his strenuous sex life, there were sometimes African jungles, where he stooped to avoid the bullets and shells as he interviewed a mercenary commander; or he was in Vietnam, with his helmet set at a jaunty angle and a correspondent's microphone in his hand, with a marvelous French song playing in the background (at this point, translucent tears welled up in Marina's eyes) as he wandered past the bodies of young American soldiers sprawled in invocation on the ground, and the fleshy-faced Frenchman was every bit as brave and sexy as they were. In short, the film was very subtle, with multiple levels of meaning, but Marina was only interested in the plot, and she sighed with relief when the hero was back in Paris, in a hotel room, with a foggy morning outside the window, and the final cheek was pressed against his reliable back.

Near the end, Marina became so engrossed in her own thoughts that she didn't notice that the magic aquarium had been extinguished and she was out on the street again. She came to her senses only when the sun blinded her eyes, and she hurried into the shade of an avenue of cypresses, measuring her favorite scenes from the movies against her own life.

There she is lying in bed, wearing a yellow silk dressing gown, and on the bedside table beside her is a basket of flowers. The telephone rings. Marina picks up the receiver and hears the fleshy-faced man's voice:

"It's me. We parted only five minutes ago, but you said I could call you any time."

"I was asleep," Marina says in a throaty voice.

"At this time of night there are hundreds of things to do in Paris," says the man.

"All right," says Marina. "But make it something original."

Or: Marina (wearing slim sunglasses) is locking her car, and the fleshy-faced man has stopped beside her and is making subtle comments on architecture. Marina raises her eyes and looks at him with cold curiosity:

"Do we know each other?"

"No," says the man, "but we would if we were living in the same hotel room . . ."

Suddenly Marina forgot the film and stopped dead.

"Where am I going?" she thought, perplexed, and looked around her.

Ahead of her was a solitary white five-story apartment building with balconies covered in ivy. In front of the building was a dusty vacant lot, crisscrossed with tire tracks, and on the edge of the lot stood a smelly white outhouse. She could also see a deserted bus stop and several blank stone walls. Marina felt with absolute certainty that she should not go in that direction, but she looked around and realized she had no reason to go back either.

"I have to do something," she thought. Something very much like amputating the wings—it seemed as though she had remembered what it was just a moment ago. She'd even walked along the lane with a vague awareness of where she was going and why, but now she'd completely forgotten. Marina felt the same yearning she'd felt on the boardwalk.

"If we were living in the same hotel room," she muttered, "in the same ho . . . ho . . . Oh, God."

She slapped her forehead. She had to begin digging a hole for her burrow.

•

She found a suitable spot close to the main building at the resort, in a wide crack between two garages, where the soil was quite damp and good for digging. Marina pushed aside the empty bottles and rusty tin cans with her shoe, opened her handbag, took out a brand-new red trowel, squatted down, and thrust it into the Crimean loam.

She managed the first few feet without any particular effort: after the layer of soil there was a layer of clay mixed with sand, which was not difficult to dig. When the top of the pit was level with her chest, she regretted that she hadn't made the burrow wider, so that it would be easier to throw out the dirt. But soon she thought of a way to make her work lighter. First she loosened the dirt under her feet thoroughly and then threw it over the edge of the pit in handfuls. Sometimes she came across broken bricks, shards from old bottles, and the rotten roots of trees cut down long ago, and this complicated things, but not very much. Marina was so engrossed in what she was doing that she didn't realize how much time had passed. As she tossed a large stone out of the pit, she was astonished to see that the sky was dark.

Eventually the pit was so deep that Marina had to stand on tiptoe as she threw out the dirt, and she sensed that it was time to dig sideways. This proved to be more difficult, because the soil here was less yielding and the trowel often scraped against stone. Marina gritted her teeth, immersed herself totally in her work, and for the next few hours there was nothing else in her world except soil, stones, and the trowel.

When she came to her senses, the first chamber was almost finished. She was surrounded by darkness, and when she crawled out of the side passage into the burrow's vertical section, the stars were twinkling overhead.

Marina felt stunned by fatigue, but she knew that on no account could she lie down or go to sleep. She clambered out of the burrow onto the ground and began scattering the soil she had dug out, so that no one would notice the entrance to the burrow. There was too much of it, however, and Marina realized that she couldn't conceal it all right there. She thought for a moment, took off her skirt, and tied the lower hem in a knot, making something like a large sack. She stuffed as much soil into it as it would hold, lifted the load onto her shoulder with a struggle, and staggered in the direction of the vacant lot. The moon was shining, and at first

Marina was afraid to come out of the shadows, but then she gathered her courage, ran quickly behind the garages, across the lot bathed in blue moonlight, and dumped the dirt by the side of the road. The second time she felt less afraid, and the third time she even stopped glancing across at the windows of the five-story building, which were lit by dim lamps or by the reflection of the moon. Her shoes prevented her from moving quickly, and the heel on one of them had broken while she was digging the burrow. Marina kicked them off; she didn't need them anymore.

It was easier to run barefoot, and quite soon the mound of dirt by the road looked as though it had been dumped by a truck, and the entrance to the burrow was no longer visible. Marina was dead on her feet, but she still had enough strength to find a piece of cardboard from a pack of cigarettes with a picture of an umbrella and the word *Parisienne* printed on it. She covered the entrance with it as she descended into the burrow. Everything was done—she'd done it.

"All right," she murmured to herself, crawling down the earth wall to the ground, remembering the fleshy-faced man from the film. "All right, but make it something original . . ."

All the next day, she slept. She only woke once for a short while, crawled to the entrance of the burrow, moved the piece of cardboard a little to one side, and glanced out. A ray of sunlight slanted in, and she could hear birds chattering, sounding so happy it seemed almost unnatural. Marina put back the cardboard and crawled back to her chamber.

When she woke up the next time, the first thing she felt was hunger. She opened the handbag that had solved all her problems so far, but all she found was a pair of slim sunglasses, just like the ones the girl in the film had worn. Marina decided to crawl outside, and then she noticed that the skirt she had used as a sack the night before was nowhere to be seen; she must have left it by the road with the final load of dirt. Marina had no shoes on her feet either; she remembered she had taken them off when they got in her way. She could not go out looking like that. Marina sat on the dirt floor and cried until she fell asleep again.

When she woke up, it was dark. Something in her had changed while she slept, and she no longer thought about whether she could or couldn't go out looking as she did. She simply groped in the darkness for the trowel, pushed aside the cardboard, climbed out, sat down, and raised her eyes to the sky.

Night in the Crimea is astonishingly beautiful. As the sky darkens, it rises away from the earth and the stars are clear and bright. The Crimea is imperceptibly transformed from the spa of the Soviet Union into a Roman province, and your heart is filled with the inexpressibly familiar feelings of all those who have ever stood on its ancient roads at night, listening to the song of the cicadas and gazing up at the sky without thinking. The straight, narrow cypresses seem like columns left behind from buildings demolished long ago; the sea murmurs exactly the same way it always has; and before you rolls your sphere of dung. You sense for a moment just how mysterious and incomprehensible life is, and how tiny a part of what life could be we actually call by that name.

Marina looked down and shook her head in an attempt to gather her thoughts. Finally she realized that she had to go to the market to see what she could find there.

She slowly approached the dark cliff face of the main hotel, lifting her feet high to avoid stumbling. She could see almost nothing, and for all her caution, her foot got caught in a hole and she fell, nearly spraining her ankle. The pain cleared her head, and Marina realized it would be much easier and safer to crawl. She went on like that until she came across a lighted path planted with flowers, and then she galloped toward the lights on the boardwalk, moving on three limbs, with one hand grasping the trowel, notched and scratched from its long and heavy duty.

The market was simply a section of the boardwalk roofed with metal sheeting. There was no one around, and Marina began rummaging behind the empty stalls, trying to find something edible. In about twenty minutes she found plenty of bruised and squashed apples and pears, a few plums, two half-eaten corn cobs, and a bunch of grapes. She put all this into a torn plastic bag she found, and went over to the empty tables beside the dead, fireless grill. She had noticed people drinking beer and eating kebabs here in the daytime, and she decided to see whether there was anything left.

"Lady, where did you get the grapes?"

Marina was so startled she almost dropped her bag. When she looked around, she was even more frightened and she sprang back several steps. In front of her stood a thin woman wearing blue shorts smeared with clay and a torn blouse. Her eyes blazed wildly, there was dirt in her matted hair, and her arms and legs were badly scratched. One hand clutched to her chest a plywood box full of leftovers, and the other held a trowel exactly like Marina's. Marina knew she was facing another ant female.

"Over there," she said, pointing in the direction of the stalls. "But there isn't any more, it's all gone."

The woman smiled sweetly and took a step toward Marina, fixing her with a burning gaze. Marina understood immediately, and she crouched down and held her trowel out in front of her. The other female threw her box on the grass, hissed, and leaped at Marina, trying to butt her in the stomach. Marina managed to block the blow with her plastic bag; then she smashed her trowel into the woman's face and kicked her hard. The ant female squealed and leaped back.

"Get out of here, you dirty beast," Marina screamed.

"Beast yourself," growled the woman, backing off. "You shameless bitches move in as though you own the place . . ."

Marina stepped toward her, waving her trowel, and the woman scurried off into the darkness. Marina bent over her box, selected a few of the best bruised tomatoes, and put them into her own plastic bag.

"Just move in . . . We'll see who's the stranger here! Ugly

bitch!" she shouted triumphantly after the woman, and set off toward the overpass; she stopped a few yards short of it, thought for a moment, then went back and picked up the box which the ugly bitch had dropped.

"How horrible she looked!" she thought with loathing.

Marina piled the food in the corner of the burrow, then crawled out again, this time toward the main hotel. She was in a very good mood.

"Yes, that's the way life is," she whispered, peering ahead into the darkness.

Finally she found what she was looking for. On the lawn there was a small pile of straw covered with a plastic sheet which Marina had noticed on the very first day. In a few trips she had dragged all the straw over to her burrow, and then, astonished and delighted at her own bravery, she stole up to the wall of the building and slowly along it, crouching as she passed the windows. One of them was open, and from inside she could hear the loud breathing of people asleep. Marina turned her head away so as not to catch sight of her reflection in the window, leaped up, and with a single graceful gesture tore down the curtain hanging on the window and dashed back to her burrow without looking back.

THE MOTH DRAWN

TO THE LIGHT

The mirror in the heavy frame of unvarnished wood that hung above the headboard looked absolutely black, reflecting the darkest wall in the room. From time to time Mitya would click his cigarette lighter, sending orange waves rippling across the surface of the mirror, but the lighter heated up very quickly and he had to put out the flame. A little light fell on the bed from the window, even though it was evening, and the music had begun playing out on the open-air dance floor. Through the net curtains he could make out distant flashes of light from colored lightbulbs, or rather, the reflections of the colored flashes on the leaves of the trees.

Mitya lay there in the semidarkness, his feet propped up on the high latticework headboard of the bed, gently stroking Marcus Aurelius Antonius, whom the centuries had compressed into a small green parallelogram which it was too dark to read. Beside Marcus Aurelius lay another book, a Chinese one, *The Evening Conversations of the Mosquitoes U and Tse*.

"It's remarkable," he thought. "The stupider the song, the more moving it is. Only whatever you do, don't start thinking about what they're singing. Otherwise, it all . . ."

Mitya was tired of lying there. He took a piece of paper covered in writing out of the book, folded it in quarters, stuck it in his pocket, and got up. He fumbled until he found his cigarettes on the table, then unlocked the door and went out. The only light in the narrow passage between the resort cottages came from his neighbor's window. He could see the gate, the bench by the fence, and the tall pale weeds in the dried-up channel of the stream. Mitya locked the door and gave a start when he saw his own reflection in the window. Ever since he realized he'd left the cocoon, he'd begun to look rather strange in the dark. The heavy wings folded behind his back looked liked a cloak of silver brocade stretching almost down to the ground, and Mitya sometimes wondered how others perceived them.

Behind the bright curtains of the next house, people were playing cards and talking. A married couple lived there, and to judge from the voices, today they had guests.

"Hearts it is," said a man's voice. "Of course, Oxana, life has changed. You keep on asking, but really everything's different now that we live together."

"But are things better or worse?" asked an insistent woman's voice.

"Well . . . Now I have responsibilities," the man's voice said thoughtfully. "I know where I have to go after work. And there's a child, you know . . . I'm playing blind."

"You're already down to minus four hundred," another male voice broke in.

"So what can I do about it?" asked the first voice. "Six of hearts."

Mitya lit a cigarette—several small insects hurtled toward the flame of his lighter—went out through the gate and jumped across the dry bed of the stream. He walked a ways carefully in darkness, scrambled past the bushes and out onto the pavement, then stopped and looked back. The bright line of the road climbed until it broke off at the top of the hill, and beyond that he could see the dark silhouettes of the mountains. From the sea, one of them, the mountain on the right, looked like a huge eagle clad in armor, with its head bent forward. From the launch that went by in the evenings, you could sometimes see mysterious lights on the summit. There was probably a lighthouse up there, but no lights were visible at the moment.

Mitya took a few more drags on his cigarette, dropped the butt on the pavement, crushed it, and began loping slowly along. After a few steps, he was caught in a current of air and carried up through the treetops. He drew in his legs to avoid snagging the electric wire stretched between two poles, and when there was nothing left above him but the clear dark sky, he began making wide circles to gain altitude. Soon it became cooler, and his back ached with fatigue. Deciding he'd climbed high enough, Mitya looked down.

Below, just like on any other evening, he saw the scattered bright points of streetlights and windows. There weren't many sources of light bright enough to arouse even a faint desire to fly toward them—only two restaurant signs, the pink neon ulcer of the SIFLIT company on the corner of the dark tower of the resort, and the flickering glow of the open-air dance floor close by. From this altitude it looked like a large open flower, constantly changing color, but instead of scent it gave off music, which could be heard even up there. Instinct drove all the insects in the area to this light every time the electricity was switched on, and Mitya decided to go down and take a look at what was happening.

When he was lower, he hedgehopped, clipping the tops of the trees. From up close, the dance floor no longer looked like a flower. It was transformed into a New Year's vision from childhood, an immense tangle of garlands of bright electric bulbs shining through the branches, from which emanated music of astonishing vulgarity and weird beauty. "Your cherry-red Lada has driven me insane," some crazy woman was singing through a dozen powerful microphones.

Keeping a careful eye on the path where he usually landed

as it rushed past beneath him, Mitya extended his wings fully, turned them against the breeze beating into his face, and hung motionless in the air. Dropping gently onto the dry hard ground, he left the path and set off across the grass.

The dance floor was simply a field paved over and surrounded by a tall fence. Set against the fence was a low wooden stage piled high with black loudspeaker boxes. Around the perimeter of the dance floor were several rows of crowded benches, and the dance floor itself was filled with writhing, steaming bodies, like a bus at rush hour. Mitya paid to go in, walked past several bottle-green flies, and sat on the end of a bench. During the evening the crowd had changed several times: when they were tired, dancers crawled back to the benches or left, but others got up to take their place and the dancing never stopped for a moment. Mitya liked to think how much like life all this was, but his satisfaction at his own detachment was clouded by an awareness that for some reason he was also sitting there on the same bench as all the others, gazing at the dancers' sweaty faces.

Suddenly the music grew louder; the lights went out and then began to flash in turn, snatching frozen figures out of the darkness for a split second, now green, now blue, now red, and in the brief moments of its existence the crowd resembled a cluster of plaster statues transported here from all the Gorky Parks and Young Pioneer camps in the country. Several minutes went by like this, and then it became clear that really there was no dance, and no dance floor, and no dancers. There was nothing but a multitude of dead Gorky Parks, each of which existed for only a split second while the lamp was lit before disappearing, to be replaced by another Gorky Park equally lifeless and deserted, differing only in the color of its temporary sky and the angles at which the statues' limbs were bent.

Mitya stood up, pushed his way through the cheerfully buzzing girls in blue and green dresses, and went out through the gates, where several musclemen were sitting in menacing, bright-colored tracksuits. Through a gap in the trees he could see the dim purple glow of a streetlight. It flared up, flickered a few times, and then went out; acting on a sudden impulse, Mitya set off into the darkness in that direction.

Soon passing the trees that concealed the sky, he came upon a tarnished green bust of Chekhov gazing thoughtfully at him out of the bushes, with the shards of a broken vodka bottle gleaming beside it in the moonlight. The sounds of cheerful voices and quiet tapping came from a group of people sitting under one of the dim streetlights, playing dominoes and drinking beer. Mitya thought he really should go for a swim, and he walked along a row of benches which offered its inviting feminine curve to the sea.

"We'll see who's the stranger here! Ugly bitch!" he heard a woman's voice shouting from the direction of the market.

Mitya lit a cigarette and saw a dark figure up ahead, leaning on the wall. He looked at its long silvery cloak and shook his head doubtfully.

"Dima!" he called.

"Mitya?" the figure said. "So you came down after all."

"We'll see who's the stranger here . . ." Mitya said, moving closer to shake the outstretched hand. "Are you waiting for someone?"

Dima shook his head.

"Shall we walk?"

Dima nodded.

They went down the creaking wooden steps to the beach, walked across the crunching gravel and found themselves facing a narrow strip of surf. A wide, straight silver road led across the sea to the moon, its color like that of a moth's wings.

"It's beautiful," said Mitya.

"Yes, it is," Dima agreed.

"Have you never wanted to fly to that light? Not just to get some fresh air, but for real, all the way to the end?"

"I did once," said Dima, "but that wasn't me."

They turned and walked slowly along the shining edge of the sea.

"Are you here on your own?"

"I'm always on my own," said Dima.

"Just recently I've noticed," said Mitya, "that frequent use makes some expressions gleam, like banisters."

"And what else have you noticed recently?" Dima asked.

Mitya thought.

"That depends what you call recently," he said. "How long has it been since we last saw each other, a year?"

"About that."

"Well, for instance, last winter I did notice one thing. That most of the time in Moscow it's dark. Not in the figurative sense, but in the actual meaning of the word. I remember I was standing in the kitchen talking on the telephone. There was a weak yellow bulb up near the ceiling. I looked out the window and it struck me how dark it was . . ."

"Yes," said Dima. "Something like that happened to me, too. And then I realized something else—that we live in this darkness all the time, only sometimes it's just a little bit brighter. Strictly speaking, you become a moth the moment you realize that you're surrounded by darkness."

"I don't know," said Mitya. "I think the way moths and butterflies are divided into night creatures and day creatures is purely arbitrary. In the final analysis, they all fly toward the light. It's instinct."

"No. We're divided into night creatures and day creatures because some of us fly toward the light and some fly toward the darkness. How can you fly toward the light, tell me, if you think you're already surrounded by light?"

"So you say all of them"—Mitya nodded toward the boardwalk—"fly toward the darkness?"

"Almost."

"What about us?"

"We fly toward the light, of course."

Mitya laughed.

"It makes you feel like some kind of conspirator," he said.

"Nonsense. They're the conspirators. Every last one of them. Even the ones playing dominoes up there."

"To be quite honest," said Dima, "I don't feel as though I'm flying toward the light just now."

"If you think we're flying somewhere, and not simply walking along the beach, then there can be no doubt you are flying into the darkness. Or rather, you're circling around a ball of dung and taking it for a lamp."

"What ball?"

"It doesn't matter," said Dima. "It's a philosophical concept."

"But what do you call light?" Mitya asked. "For me, it's as though there used to be something in life that was amazingly simple and more important than anything else, and then it disappeared and we've only just realized it ever existed. And it turns out that absolutely everything we ever used to want only made sense because there was this most important thing. And, without it, we don't want anything at all. And we can't even give it a name. Do you know what light I'd really like to fly toward? There was this verse, listen: 'No regrets have I for life's anguished breathing, for what are life and death? But I regret that light that shone above the universe, and now weeps in the night as it recedes' . . ."

"I don't think you ought to feel sorry for that light. It would be more appropriate for that light to feel sorry for you. Or do you think you yourself are the light that weeps in the darkness?"

"Perhaps I do."

"Then don't go into the darkness," said Dima. "No one's forcing you."

A new song started up from the dance floor—a woman sadly asking the dark sky, the moon, and two dark figures wandering along a beach where she was today, and complaining that she did not know where to find either herself or anyone else. The last line was inaudible, but that wasn't important, because it wasn't the words that mattered, or even the music, but something else—the fact that everything around them was meditating in infinite sadness on where it

was today, and how it could possibly find either itself or anyone else.

"Like it?" asked Mitya.

"Not bad," said Dima. "The best thing is that she doesn't
understand what she's singing about. Just like your friend,
who couldn't find anything better to do than to feel sorry for
the light receding into the darkness."

"He's not my friend," said Mitya.

"Good," said Dima. "I wouldn't want to have anything to
do with someone like that, either. You know, everything that
rouses the pity of the dead is based on a very simple mechanism. For instance, if you show a dead man a fly stuck on
flypaper with music playing, and you make him think for a
second that this fly is him, then he'll burst into tears out of
compassion for his fellow corpse."

"So that means I'm dead, too?" asked Mitya.

"Of course," said Dima, "you must be. But at least I can
explain it to you, and that means you're not totally dead."

They went back up onto the boardwalk. The domino players had disappeared and all that was left of them was a newspaper fluttering in the wind, a few wooden boxes, some empty
beer bottles, and the bony remains of a few fish; the melancholy induced by the music made it seem as though they
hadn't all simply gone home but had dissolved into the surrounding darkness. All that was needed to make the impression complete were their weathered skeletons lying beside the
bottles and the fish bones.

"What was that you were saying about the dance floor?"
asked Dima.

"I was there just now. I even went in and sat down for a
while. It was very strange. I seemed to see they were all dead,
nothing but plaster models. You know that toy with the two
wooden bears and the hammers? You move a wooden stick
backward and forward and they hammer on the anvil?"

"Yes."

"Well, it's just the same up there. They all dance and laugh and greet each other, and then you look down and you can see the beams moving under the floor. Backward and forward."

"So what?"

"What do you mean, so what? They were all flying toward the light, after all. Whichever way you fly, there's only the dance floor that actually shines, and it turns out that everyone thinks they're flying toward life, but all they find is death. That is, at any given moment they move toward the light but still find themselves in darkness. You know, if I wrote a novel about insects, that's how I'd represent their life: a village by the sea, darkness, and a few lamps shining in the darkness above this repulsive dancing. And everyone flies to this light, because there's nothing else. But to fly to those lamps means . . ."

Mitya snapped his fingers, searching for the right word.

"I don't know how to explain."

"You already have," said Dima. "When you were talking about the moon. The moon is the biggest dance floor of all. It's absolutely the same thing. It's not the real light."

"No," said Mitya. "The light is real. Light is always real, if you can see it."

"True," said Dima. "The light is real. But where does it come from?"

"What do you mean? It comes from the moon."

"Yes? Did you never have the idea that the moon is actually totally black?"

"I think I'd call it yellowish-white," said Mitya, looking up attentively. "Or slightly bluish."

"All right. Of course, five billion flies will agree with you. But you're not a fly. The fact that you see a yellow spot when you look at the moon doesn't actually mean that it is yellow. I can't see why nobody can understand that. The answer to all your questions is hanging right there over your head."

"Perhaps," said Mitya. "Unfortunately, none of these questions come up for me. But I understand what you're saying.

You're trying to tell me that when I look at the moon I see the light of the sun which it reflects, but it doesn't shine itself. I don't think that's important—it's enough for me that the light exists. And when I see it, the most important part of me makes me move toward the light. Where it comes from, or what kind of light it is, is not particularly important."

"All right. You don't want to fly toward the moon. What light are you moving toward at the moment?"

"The nearest streetlight."

"And then where?"

"The next one."

Dima stretched out his hand, made a movement as though throwing an invisible switch, and suddenly all the lamps on the boardwalk went out. Mitya stopped.

"What light are you moving toward now?" Dima asked.

"That's some trick. How did you do it?"

"Just the way you were thinking," said Dima. "I arranged for an electrician to sit in the bushes and wait for my signal. And all just to make an impression on you."

"Is that what I was thinking?"

"Weren't you?"

"More or less. I did think about the electrician and the sign, but not about the bushes. Will you tell me how you do it?"

"What? How I read minds?"

"No, no, I can do that myself. Other people's minds are easy to read. I meant the streetlights."

"It's very simple. Once you've answered a single question, you can control all kinds of light."

"What question?" asked Mitya.

"It's really best to ask yourself the question, but since you're not inclined to do that, I'll ask it for you."

Dima paused.

"The moon reflects the sun's light," he said. "But what light does the sun reflect?"

Mitya sat down on a bench without speaking and leaned back.

It was quiet. The wind rustled the leaves over their heads, and the rumble of the sea mingled with the final notes of a fading song. It seemed that the mixture of sounds was coming from the yellow disk hanging in the sky above the dance floor. Then it was joined by the roar of a tourist launch approaching its mooring, and to their left the waves from its wake slowly rolled into sight.

"American boy, I'm leaving with you, leaving with you, Moscow, goodbye," two pure young voices screeched out over the dance floor, and then they heard balalaikas playing an accompaniment, as naïve and touching as a Girl Scout's sash.

THE THIRD ROME

The tiny hang glider hurtled past so close to the jagged rocks protruding from the mountainside that for an instant it nearly merged with its own shadow, and everyone at the tables in the open-air café gasped in unison. Slipping through the sky like a silvery moth, the triangle swerved away at the last moment and flew out over the sea toward the beach. Sam applauded, and Arthur looked over at him.

"Do you find it that impressive?" he asked.

"In my younger days," said Sam, "I used to do something similar, so I can appreciate another person's skill. I would never have gone that close to the cliff."

"I just can't understand the point of risking your life so senselessly," said Arthur.

"If you think about it, you and I also risk our lives every day," said Sam.

"Yes, but you know quite well that's because we have to. I wouldn't like to splatter my brains against a cliff."

"True enough," said Sam, following the movements of the triangle thoughtfully as it turned back toward the jagged rocks. "True enough. Where do they start from?"

"That hill over there," said Arthur. "See it?"

Far beyond the beach and the village there was a low mountain, long and flat, and on its peak they could make out several colorful hang gliders. Sam took out a small brown notebook and jotted something down, making a rough sketch of the beach, the village, and the low mountain.

"There's always an upcurrent there," said Arthur. "That's why they're so fond of it."

A waitress with a face as dour as fate came over to them. Without speaking, she unloaded plates, a bottle of champagne, and glasses from her tray. Sam looked up at her in bewilderment and then turned his eyes away: there was a huge crimson patch of ringworm on her cheek.

"We ordered it," Arthur explained.

"Ah," said Sam. "I'd forgotten."

"This is classed as a restaurant," said the waitress. "You can see the rules if you like. Waiting up to forty minutes."

Sam nodded absentmindedly and looked at his plate. On the menu the dish had a Ukrainian name, country beef stew with onion. It consisted of a few small triangular pieces of meat lying in strict architectural formation, a sea of sauce to the right of the meat, and a low mountain of mashed potatoes, decorated with several colorful specks of carrot and dill. The potatoes were flowing like lava toward the meat, making the contents of the plate look like a bird's-eye view of Pompeii, and at the same time they were somehow reminiscent of the panoramic view of the small seaside town from the restaurant table. Sam raised his fork and held it over his plate, and then he noticed a young fly sitting on the edge between the potato and the sauce—at first he'd taken her for a bit of dill. He slowly held out his hand toward her. The fly trembled, but she didn't fly away. He carefully took her between his finger and thumb and set her on an empty chair.

The fly was very young. Her firm green skin glittered gaily in the sunlight, and Sam thought how precise the name "greenbottle" was. Her limbs were covered with dark hairs and ended in delicate pink suckers, as if two half-open mouths waited invitingly on each of her palms, and her waist was so slim that she looked as though the slightest breath of wind could break her in two. The shyly fluttering wings, looking like two sheets of mica glimmering with all the colors of the rainbow, were covered with the standard pattern of dark lines: no special skill in wing reading was required to read her simple fate in them. Her eyes were also green, with a slightly sullen look, and a long dark fringe fell down over them from her forehead, making the fly appear even younger than she was and creating the impression of a schoolgirl dressed up in her older sister's dress.

Catching Sam's eye, she blushed slightly. "How are you?" she asked in English, enunciating the words painstakingly. "I'm Natasha. And what is your name?"

"Sam Sacker," answered Sam. "But we can talk Russian."

Natasha smiled, displaying her even white teeth, looked over at Arthur's scornful face, and was instantly gloomy again.

"Am I bothering you?" she asked, and shifted on her chair as though she was about to get up.

"Well, how can I put it?" muttered Arthur, looking away.

"Not at all," Sam cut in quickly. "How could such an enchanting being possibly bother anyone? A bit of bubbly?"

"With pleasure," Natasha replied, and she grasped the glass proffered by Sam between her finger and thumb.

"Do you live here?" Sam asked.

Natasha took a sip of the sparkling wine and nodded.

"Were you born here?"

"No," said Natasha. "I was born very far away, in the north."

"What do you do?"

"I play music," answered Natasha. She put her glass on the table and moved her hands and arms as though stretching a chest expander.

"Yes?" said Sam, moving his eyes from the two mounds under the gleaming green cloth of Natasha's dress to the cheap silver bracelet between her sucker and her wrist. "I'd like to hear you play sometime."

"Excuse me," said Arthur. "Do you mind if I go make a phone call? Arnold's been gone a long time."

Sam nodded, and Arthur went over to the phone booth squeezed between two kiosks. There was a line for the phone. Arthur took his place and began looking over the books laid out on the lawn by the street venders.

Natasha opened the handbag lying on her knees, took out a small file, looked at it in astonishment, tossed it back, and fished out some makeup. "Where are you from, Sam?" she asked, looking at herself in the mirror. "Are you American?"

"Yes," answered Sam. "But it's hard to say where I live—I spend most of the time flying backward and forward."

"Are you a businessman?"

Natasha opened a tube of lipstick and painted the suckers on her hands, and Sam thought this made her look vulgar, but twice as attractive.

"You could say that," he answered. "But what interests me most of all in life are new impressions."

"And are there lots of new impressions here?"

"Enough," said Sam. "But, you know, they're for fans."

A shadow fell across the table, and suddenly there was a smell totally out of place for early autumn, an intense scent of wildflowers and trees in bloom.

Glancing around, Natasha saw a short, fat man in a colorful T-shirt glaring at Sam with hatred as he toyed with a small dark case.

"Arnold!" said Sam happily. "We've been waiting for you. Arthur went to phone you. Did you find anything out?"

"Yes, I did," Arnold replied, throwing the case onto the chair beside Sam. "Now I know everything."

"You found it!" said Sam, picking up the case. "Thank God for that. I didn't notice you were carrying it. Thank you."

He opened the case and ran his eye over the contents, then put his thumb and forefinger together and showed Arnold a ring of emptiness about the size of a silver dollar. The fat man pulled over a chair from the next table and sat down heavily.

"This is Natasha," said Sam. "Natasha, this is Arnold."

Arnold turned toward Natasha and glared piercingly at her.

"I see," he said, when he'd seen enough. "Why don't you try working at some factory? Or don't you care for that?"

"What are you talking about?" whispered Natasha, turning pale. Her nose was stung by the sharp smell of eau de cologne. She looked over at Sam in puzzlement and saw the smile fading from his face and an expression of horror in his eyes.

"Don't frighten the girl," he said, glancing toward Arthur, who was on his way back from the telephone booth. "He's only joking, Natasha."

"Me, joking? You come here to drink blood, you bastard, and you think we're going to waste our time on jokes?"

"Who's 'we'?" asked Sam.

"I'll tell you," said Arnold, getting up from his chair. There's no way of knowing what would have happened next if Arthur hadn't run up and smashed the wine bottle over his head.

Arnold tumbled to the floor and lay there, not moving. Conversation at the nearby tables stopped, and several people rose from their seats, preparing either to get involved or to run away. Arthur quickly sat astride his colleague and tried to pull his arms behind his back, which proved not to be so easy, even though Arnold didn't seem to offer any resistance.

"I knew he wouldn't be able to resist," Arthur muttered nervously. "I knew he'd have to try it. And he said you were psychologically unstable. You go, before he comes to his senses. Take the girl with you. And I . . ."

Arnold stirred, and Arthur almost fell to the ground.

"Let's go, Natasha," said Sam, taking her by the arm.

They quickly got up from the table and walked away, passing a militiaman running toward the scene of the fight.

"What's wrong with him? Drugs?" asked Natasha.

"Something like that," answered Sam. "I don't like discussing other people's misfortunes. Do you know anywhere we can get a bite to eat? We never did get anything here."

Natasha looked back at the crowd packed in between the tables at the restaurant.

"It's over," she said. "They've got cuffs on the jerk. What were you saying? Somewhere to eat? There's a place down by the sea; we have to take a taxi."

"I'm sorry, Natasha," said Sam. "Maybe you have other plans?"

Natasha's answer was to glance at Sam with a simple-hearted frankness that instantly made her plans quite obvious.

•

The road they were walking along ran past a deep foundation pit with the ruins of an unfinished building. Grass, bushes, and even young trees grew in the cracks in the walls, and the place looked less like a foundation dug for a new building than like a grave for a building that had died, or the excavated remains of an ancient city. Sam took a long look at it and walked on without speaking. Natasha also was silent.

"Yes," said Sam, when the pit was behind them. "That's really fascinating. One odd thing I've noticed here. They say Russia's the Third Rome, right?"

"Yes, that's right, the third. And the second Israel. Ivan the Terrible said that. I read it in the newspaper."

"Well, if we write Third Rome in Russian, *Trety Rim*, and then turn the word for 'Rome' backward, we get *Trety Mir*, Third World."

"In Yalta, about three hours from here by launch, there are cable cars. You get in on the ground level and go up to the top of the mountain. They were building a palace of culture or a Lenin museum or something up there, and then they abandoned it, and there's nothing left but the columns and part of the roof. It's huge, just standing there with nothing else near it, like a shrine or something. That's the Third Rome for you. Tell me, Sam, have you been to the first one?"

Sam nodded, and Natasha sighed.

"We're here," she said. "Now we have to find a car."

The paved path ended at a long building of indeterminate nature, in front of which two guards dressed in Adidas sweat suits were warming themselves in the sun. Under the shelter at the bus stop across the way, a few skinny, sunburned old southern women were flashing the whites of their eyes at one another. Natasha raised her hand, and an antiquated gray Volga with a reindeer mascot on its hood emerged from the shadows of the willow trees growing beside the bus stop. Natasha leaned down to the window and consulted the driver, then turned to Sam and nodded.

The driver had a long ginger mustache which stuck out asymmetrically to the sides, as though he'd just finished feeling something with it, and the car smelled of gasoline and overripe fruit. Weaving its way between small white houses drowning in a sea of green apple and pear trees, the Volga finally emerged onto a dusty dirt road. The driver revved the car up to top speed, and the landscape outside the rear window disappeared behind clouds of yellow dust, generous quantities of which also came in through the windows.

Sam coughed, covering his mouth with his hand, and Natasha saw his lips extending into a long tube. Pretending that he was picking something up off the floor, he leaned toward the back of the driver's seat, winked conspiratorially at Natasha, and put a finger to his extended lips to tell her not to say anything. Natasha nodded. The sharp point of Sam's proboscis slid gently through the gray covering of the seat. The driver shuddered. His eyes glanced uneasily at the passengers in the rear-view mirror.

"Do you really think this is the Third World, Sam?" Natasha asked, trying to distract the driver.

"Pretty much," Sam mumbled, not straightening up. "No

insult intended. Unless, of course, people are insulted by facts."

"It's just kind of a new idea."

"You'll have to get used to it. It's the geopolitical reality. Russia's a very poor country. And so is Ukraine. A place where—what's that expression?—the earth won't bear fruit. Even if we take the most fertile soil in the Kuban, it still can't compare with the earth in, say, Ohio . . ."

Sam pronounced the word "Oh-hai-oh," and it sounded as though it could be spread on bread in place of butter, making it instantly clear just how fertile the land was there.

"It's not the Third World," the driver said bitterly. "We've been sold down the river, every last one of us. Along with the rockets and the fleet. They've sucked us dry."

"Who sold us?" Natasha asked. "And who to?"

"We all know who," the driver said with absolute hatred. "Never mind the fleet, they've sold our honor . . ."

Sam mumbled something, and the driver waved his hand. "A knife in the back, you know what I mean," he muttered and fell silent.

Gradually his face turned very pale, and his eyes, which were restless and watchful, took on a glazed, indifferent look. In contrast, Sam's cheeks flushed red, as though he'd just stepped out of the sauna. He pulled his lips out of the seat, straightened up, and smiled at Natasha. Natasha maintained a studied silence.

"Natasha, have I offended you?" Sam asked.

"How?" she asked in surprise.

"With this Third World."

"Of course not, Sam. It's just that I had my fortune told when I was a child and they warned me to beware of the Roman numeral III. But I'm not afraid of it, not in the least. And I've got no reason to be offended. I'm not Russia. I'm Natasha."

"Natasha," said Sam, "is a lovely name."

There were vineyards along both sides of the road. When

the vineyards ended, the sea appeared on the left. Sam took a small glass jar from his briefcase, spat some red liquid into it, then screwed on the lid and tossed it back into the case.

•

Natasha was deep in thought, and a lovely curving wrinkle appeared on her forehead. Sam caught her eye and smiled. "Everything okay?" he asked.

"Uhn huh," said Natasha with a smile. "I was just thinking. If the first world is America, Japan, and Europe, and the Third Rome, I mean Third World, is us, Africa, and Poland, then where's the second world?"

"The second world?" Sam asked in surprise. "I don't know. That's an interesting question. I must find out where the expression comes from. There probably isn't any second world."

He glanced out the window and noticed a silver triangle high up in the sky. It could have been the same hang glider he'd watched from the restaurant, or another like it.

"There's something else I don't understand," he said. "Where are we going?"

"To get some lunch," said Natasha.

"I'm full," said Sam.

"Then maybe we should pull up here?" Natasha suggested. "It's very wild and beautiful. We can go for a swim."

Sam gulped. "Listen," he said to the driver, "I think we'll get out here, okay?"

"It's up to you," said the driver morosely. "Just give me the five dollars you promised."

Sam got out onto the road and reached into his pocket for his wallet.

"Want any *matryoshka* dolls?" asked the driver.

"What kind?" asked Sam.

"All sorts. Gorbachev, Yeltsin, Rutskoi, Mikhalkov."

Sam shook his head.

"If your back itches," he said as he handed a five-dollar bill through the open door, "rub it with eau de cologne."

The driver nodded sullenly. The car turned, spraying them

with yellow dust, and hurtled back the way it had come. Suddenly it was quiet. Sam and Natasha walked along a path that zigzagged down a steep rocky slope. They went down the hill without talking, because the path was very narrow and they had to move carefully.

Down below there was no clear shoreline; the slope ran into a labyrinth of rocks, with the sea splashing between them. Natasha took off her shoes, and Sam was touched to see she was actually wearing household slippers, and not slightly odd high-fashion shoes, as he had thought at first. Then she waded into the water up to her knees. Sam rolled up his trousers, took off his shoes and socks, and followed her, holding his case and his moccasins above his head, trying to remember what Greek legend all this reminded him of. They wended their way along the rocky shore until they came out on a large slanting slab, which protruded a few feet out of the water.

"I used to sunbathe here," said Natasha, clambering onto the rock. "You can dive from that side, it's deep there."

Sam climbed on the rock and took out his camcorder.

"Help me, Sam," said Natasha.

Sam turned and saw that she was standing with her back to him, reaching behind her for the lace fastenings of her dress. Carefully placing the camera on his moccasins, Sam stretched out and touched Natasha, and felt her tremble beneath her dress. The laces actually fastened nothing at all, and were simply, as Sam recalled from an article in *National Geographic*, a naïve device used by Russian girls to attract men. Even the metal balls on the ends of the laces looked like lures, but the tremor that ran down Natasha's back made Sam forget all about the rules of correct behavior recommended by the magazine, and when Natasha stepped out of her dress and stood there in a minuscule bathing suit of glittering green, his hands reached out for the camera of their own accord.

He spent a long time filming Natasha's thin childlike body, her happy smile, and her hair waving in the wind. He made shots of her head on the surface of the emerald water and her wet footprints on the rock. Then he gave Natasha the camera and explained what to press, dived into the water and set off at a clip toward the white spot of a tourist launch that had appeared in the distance, swimming with a butterfly stroke so reckless he almost seemed to be trying to overtake it.

When he came back to the rock, breathing heavily, Natasha was lying on her back, shielding her eyes from the sun. Sam settled himself beside her, set his cheek against the stone's warm surface, and screwed up his eyes as he looked at her.

"When I get home," he said, "I'll watch all this on TV and feel sad."

"Sam," said Natasha, "I know you've been to Rome. Have you been to France, too?"

"Yes, just recently," said Sam, moving closer. "Why do you ask?"

"Oh," said Natasha, "my mother was always talking about France. What were you doing there?"

"The usual thing, sucking blood."

"That's not what I meant. Did you go just because you felt like it?"

"Not exactly. Some friends invited me to the annual Proust festival in Combray."

"What kind of festival is that?"

Sam didn't answer for a long time, and Natasha decided he couldn't be bothered. They heard the throbbing motor of the tourist launch, and then closer at hand a few chords on a guitar, followed by a soft buzzing, and Natasha felt a faint prick on her leg. She automatically slapped the spot with her open hand, and something squashed wetly under her fingers.

Sam suddenly began speaking in a singsong voice, pronouncing some sounds with a twang through his nose. "Imagine a small village church, five centuries old, with rough-hewn statues of Christian kings gazing out onto a square where the leafless branches of chestnut trees gleam metallically in the light of a few streetlights. In front of the portal stands a solitary man with a mustache, looking like a target from a provincial shooting gallery, and then it's hard to say what happens, when an irresistible attraction steals from memory the moment of its flight, leaving only the brief contact of hands wandering at random over the silk scarf smelling of eau de cologne and cigar smoke and the coarse . . ."

"Sam," whispered Natasha, "what are you doing? Someone will see us . . ."

". . . somehow insulting sensation of the closeness of someone else's skin to your mouth. The pleasure intensifies when, behind the torn curtains of the shrouds separating one body from another, you begin to discern a muffled sound, at first the streaming of blood . . ."

"Ah, Sam . . . Not there . . ."

". . . and afterwards, the imperious heartbeats, like signals from the planet Mars or from some other world equally hidden from our sight. Their rhythm defines the movements of your body, now passionate, now mocking, and your entire consciousness seems to flow into its enduring projection, wandering in the pulsating labyrinths of another's flesh. Then suddenly it is all over, and once again you are wandering somewhere across the old stones on the surface of the road . . ."

"Sam . . ."

Sam threw himself back onto the stone and for a while he felt absolutely nothing, as though he had turned into a part of the sun-heated rock. Natasha squeezed his hand. He half opened his eyes and saw two large faceted hemispheres just in front of his face. They glittered in the sunlight like the shards of a broken bottle, and the short springy whiskers surrounding the shaggy proboscis between them were twitching.

"Sam," whispered Natasha, "is there a lot of shit in America?"

Sam smiled, nodded, and closed his eyes. The sun shone directly on his eyelids, and through them he could see a faint purple glow that he wanted to keep staring at forever and ever.

A LIFE FOR THE TSAR

It was hard to tell how many days Marina spent deepening her burrow and digging the second chamber. Days exist only where the sun rises and sets, but Marina lived and worked in total darkness. At first she had to grope her way around, but after a while she noticed that she could see quite well in the dark. She realized it quite unexpectedly, after the big bed of straw was laid out in the main chamber, covered with the stolen curtain. Marina was just thinking there should be a basket of flowers beside the bed, like in the film, when she noticed the plywood box she had taken, standing in the corner. She looked around and realized she could see everything else, too—the bed, the recess in the floor where she had stored the food from the market, and her own limbs. It was all colorless and slightly blurred, but distinctly visible.

"Probably I could see in the dark before, but I just didn't notice," thought Marina.

She picked up the box and placed it by the bed, stuck a clump of straw into it, and made it look as much like a bouquet as she could. She went to the opposite wall of the chamber and looked at the interior with approval, then went back to bed and dived under the curtain.

Something was missing. Marina struggled with her thoughts for a few minutes until she understood what it was. Then she pulled the handbag toward her, took out the slim sunglasses, and stuck them on her nose. All she had to do now was wait for the telephone to ring. There was no telephone in Marina's burrow, but she knew that the call would come one way or another, because that distant sunny morning on the boardwalk life had given her its word of honor.

Marina was warm and comfortable under the curtain, but it was a little boring. At first she tried thinking about this and that, and then, without realizing it, she slipped into a daze.

She was roused by a noise from beyond the wall. Marina was quite sure it came from beyond the wall; she had grown accustomed to the sounds that reached her from above—voices, footsteps, and the roaring engine of a car pulling out of a garage—and she automatically filtered them out, so they didn't disturb her sleep. This sound was different—someone was definitely digging in the earth beyond the wall. Marina could even hear the clang of a trowel as it struck against the stones that had caused her so much trouble earlier. Sometimes the noise faded away, but then it would start up again, closer than before, and Marina stopped worrying. Sometimes she heard singing, too: Marina couldn't make out the words, but it was clearly a man's voice, and the melody sounded like "Midnight in Moscow." Gradually the certainty crystallized within her that someone was digging their way to her, and she could even guess who it was, but a prudent apprehension prevented her from believing this completely. Leaping up from the bed, she ran over to the wall and held her ear against it, then dashed back to bed and lay still under the curtain. Whenever the noise died away, Marina was thrown into consternation.

"What if he misses and ends up digging his way to that ugly bitch?" she thought.

She remembered the ant female from the market, and her fists tightened in fury.

"And that ugly bitch will tell him that she's me. And he'll believe her, he's so stupid . . ."

The thought of so vile a deceit took her breath away, and she began imagining what she would do with that bitch if she encountered her again.

Things went on like this for quite a long time, until finally the wall beyond which the digging was going on started to shake and lumps of earth began tumbling to the floor. Marina took a last look around her chamber. Everything seemed to be in order, and she dived back under the curtain. Someone began beating on the other side of the wall, and before Marina had time to adjust the glasses on her nose, the wall caved in.

A boot appeared in the hole. It kicked at the earth several times, widening the entrance, then disappeared, and suddenly a fleshy face emerged. Marina recognized it immediately: it was him, or almost him, only his hair wasn't brown, it was ginger, and instead of a sheepskin coat he was wearing a military coat dusted with snow and featuring a major's lapels. Carefully, so he wouldn't get dirt on himself, he squeezed his way through the hole, and Marina saw he had a heavy black accordion case hanging on his chest.

"Good day to you," said the major. He took off his accordion, set the safety catch, and put it on the floor. "Are you bored here?"

Marina's stomach was tied in knots, but she found the strength to raise her sunglasses elegantly and glance at the major with cool interest.

"Are we acquainted?" she asked.

"We will be in a minute," said the major, walking up to the bed and grasping in his strong hands the edge of the curtain hanging down from the pile of straw.

•

"You just can't imagine, Nikolai, what vicious beasts there are out there," Marina said, snuggling up against the cold shaggy form lying beside her. "Just recently I went to the market to get some food and I nearly got killed. I don't know how I managed to get home afterwards. Nikolai, are you asleep?"

Nikolai didn't answer, and Marina turned over on her back and gazed up at the ceiling. She felt sleepy. Soon the ceiling seemed to disappear, and the stars began to shine overhead. One of the stars blinked and began creeping across the ceiling. Remembering the faces of the children on the poster with the images of a faded future, Marina made a wish.

.

"I'm a military man," Nikolai was saying, "a major. I live and work in the city of Magadan. But the most important thing in my life is music, so if you like music, we are sure to become very close . . ."

Marina opened her eyes. It was dark, as usual, but she knew the only morning that there is in a burrow had arrived.

"Now, Marina," Nikolai continued, "you will soon be so big that you won't be able to go out at all. But in Magadan there are hundreds of things to do in the evening, so I suggest that today we should go to the theater and have some fun."

"All right," said Marina, with a sweet pain in her heart. "But make it something original."

In place of an answer, Nikolai held out two pieces of paper, on which Marina read "The Magadan October 1993 Revolution Military Opera House"; she turned the tickets over and saw the words "A Life for the Tsar" printed in blue.

"Where is Magadan?" she asked.

Nikolai nodded toward the hole he had made in the wall, and Marina seemed to feel a draft of cold air from it.

Before the evening came, Nikolai climbed onto Marina again several times. She paid close attention to her sensations as the cold damp body heaved to and fro on top of her, and she wondered whether this could really be what all the fuss was about, and what they wrote such beautiful songs about in France. Sometimes Nikolai would stop moving and start telling her about his life in the army, what he did and who his friends were. Marina soon knew them all by name and rank. Every time Nikolai climbed down off her, he began doing things around the burrow. First he deepened the recess for the food, then he began closing off the exit leading to the two garages. For no particular reason, Marina felt depressed.

"Why are you doing that?" she asked from the bed.

"There's a draft," said Nikolai. "A strong one."

"But how will we get out?"

Nikolai nodded again toward the hole in the wall through which he had appeared a few hours earlier. By evening he had managed to make the hole an exact square and even to weave a small mat out of straw which he set on the floor in front of it.

Eventually Nikolai glanced at his watch and said: "Time to go to the theater."

Marina climbed out of bed and immediately remembered that she had absolutely nothing to wear.

"Wrap yourself in the curtain," said Nikolai when she explained the problem. "Everybody dresses like that these days."

Marina took his advice, and the result was not bad at all. Nikolai pulled on his boots, put on his coat, hung the accordion over his shoulder, and ducked through the dark hole in the wall. Marina followed him. The hole led into a long, crooked corridor, cold and dark, which ended in a narrow hole in the roof. Pale blue light and occasional snowflakes fell onto the corridor through the hole. Nikolai climbed up and held out his hand to Marina. She followed him, holding the curtain closed at the throat.

They found themselves in a dimly lit yard, from which they emerged onto a wide snow-covered embankment. Beyond the wall lay the smooth white surface of the frozen sea. The embankment was lit by a few streetlights, and there were people walking along it, mostly officers bearing accordions, some arm-in-arm with their wives, who were wrapped in curtains. Marina was relieved when she saw them. All the officers' wives were barefoot, too, and Marina stopped worrying about her appearance altogether. She took Nikolai's arm and walked along the street with him, admiring the falling snow.

The theater was a majestic gray building with columns, very much like the main building at the resort. Marina remembered the southern night, the stars in the sky, and the sound of the sea, and she shook her head—it all seemed so far away and so unreal. But the theater really did remind her of the building beside which she had once dug out her burrow, and even the plaster sheaves of wheat on the pediment were just the same, only now most of them were hidden by broad strips of red calico with an inscription in white: *Ant Is Beetle, Cricket, and Dragonfly to His Fellow Ant.*

The theater was crowded, and there was an aura of solemn festivity. The other officers' wives cast approving glances at Marina's curtain, and Marina was gratified to realize that it was as good as most of the offers. Of course, there were some that were better—one general's wife was wearing a crimson velvet drape with gold tassels, but then she was quite old and wrinkled. Nikolai introduced Marina to some of his friends, ginger-haired majors like himself, and from the moist inviting look in their eyes she knew she was making an impression.

An old general with mandibles worn down by age stopped close to Marina and glanced at her with a benevolent smile. Marina thought she should talk to him about culture.

"Please tell me," she said. "Do you like French films?"

"No," the general replied with military terseness. "I don't like French films. I like the films of Sergei Solovyev, especially where they hit him on the head with a brick and he falls off his stool to the floor."

Marina realized that what she had taken for a benevolent smile was actually the result of paralysis of the facial muscles, and the general's look was not one of benevolence at all, but one of fear.

"Your husband," added the general, with a sideways glance at Nikolai, "is a good officer with good prospects."

"I serve the Magadan Anthill!" Nikolai said, drawing himself to attention and pinching Marina's leg so that she wouldn't think of saying anything else.

The bell rang, and they crowded into the auditorium. Nikolai and Marina did not have very good seats and looked onto the stage from a distant angle. They couldn't make out what was happening at the back, and when the performance began, Marina just couldn't figure out what it was about. Nikolai leaned over to her and began to explain in a whisper that the big black ants had attacked the red ants' anthill, and one old ant who had promised to lead them to the chamber where the queen lay with her eggs actually led them into the ant lion's tunnel. People began shushing Nikolai and he stopped, but now Marina knew what was going on.

She could hear most of the action, but when the climax came and the old ant and the ant lion were left alone on the stage, Marina had a good view. The ant lion was a ruddy-faced individual with a shaved head, wearing the military uniform of the twenties with a medal on his chest. He sat on a chair, slapping his gray astrakhan hat against his leg in obvious boredom as he waited for the old ant to finish singing. Eventually the old ant was silent and crawled to the back, and the ant lion stood up and followed him. The orchestra struck chords of alarm and terror, and a gasp ran through the audience, but Marina couldn't see a thing. She stared at the heavy green stage curtain and dreamed of Nikolai's becoming a general and getting a curtain like that for her.

When the performance was over, Nikolai suggested they go to the buffet for a glass of champagne, and Marina happily agreed. She remembered that in the film the fleshy-faced man always drank champagne from tall narrow glasses with his women. Then disaster struck.

On the empty stairway Nikolai stumbled, lost his balance, and fell, striking the back of his head on one of the steps. He lost consciousness; his legs began jerking rapidly and a distressed look appeared on his face. Marina tried to lift him by the arm, but Nikolai was too heavy, and she dashed down the stairs to call for help. Fortunately, on the next landing she came across two of the majors Nikolai had introduced as his friends before the performance. They were smoking in silence as they waited in line for the buffet. When Marina told them what had happened, they threw down their cigarettes and hurried after her.

Nikolai was lying in the same position, his legs still jerking, but now his arms had begun to move involuntarily, too. They were performing smooth sideways movements, as though he was playing his accordion, but what scared Marina most was the fact that Nikolai was humming "Midnight in Moscow."

One of the majors squatted down beside Nikolai and took his pulse, while the other timed it with his watch. After a minute or so they exchanged glances, and the one who was taking the pulse—all the while Nikolai's free arm continued to play the accordion—shook his head.

Both majors looked at Marina, and for the first time she noticed the terrible mandibles moving to and fro under their noses. In fact, Nikolai and she herself had mandibles which were exactly the same, but she had never thought about it before. Tears clouded Marina's vision, and through this dim veil she saw a large dark object being held out to her. She held out her hands, and the accordion in its case was placed in them. She felt paralyzed, and she watched apathetically as the first major raised Nikolai's leg and the second quickly gnawed it off with his mandibles. The thin red stripe along the trouser leg jerked in time with the movements of his jaws. When he gnawed off the other leg, several more majors appeared. They set their glasses of champagne on the floor, and the job began to go more quickly. Nikolai stopped playing his invisible accordion only when one of the new arrivals gnawed at his neck and obviously bit through a nerve. Another major brought a pile of old copies of the newspaper *Magadan Ant* and began to wrap Nikolai's severed limbs in them. After that, there was a long gap in Marina's memory.

The cold snowflakes pricking her face brought her to her senses on the street. The theater was far behind her. In one hand she was carrying the accordion in its box, and in the other she had two long, heavy bundles, wrapped tightly in several layers of newspaper. Somehow she managed to reach the point where their outing had begun a few hours earlier, and she spotted the two rusty garages standing at an angle to each other at the back of the snow-covered yard. Between the garages she could see a round depression under a thin layer of snow, and recent footprints. Marina felt under the snow, removed the cover, which was the side of a North Star cigarette pack, from the entrance to the tunnel, and went in.

Back in her burrow, it was dark and quiet. Marina set her bundles down in the snow that had drifted in, and crawled off to bed. Only when she had scrambled onto the pile of straw did she recall what had happened at the theater when they had almost finished cutting Nikolai up. Unable to watch anymore, she had turned away, and then she had seen the ugly bitch from the market coming down the carpeted staircase, arm in arm with a tall ginger-haired colonel in gleaming boots; she was wearing a fixed look of triumph and was draped in a lemon-colored curtain patterned with purple bunches of grapes.

IN MEMORY OF

MARCUS AURELIUS

The tourist launch was well out to sea, traveling in a straight line as though it were heading for Turkey. On the left, the shoreline, previously hidden by the mountain, jutted out into the sea, and though the shore itself was not visible, there were glimpses of lights. They seemed to be shining on the surface of the sea, like candles drifting past in paper boxes floating on small rafts. The moon, too, looked like a paper lantern lit by a candle, hanging among clouds which were scattered thinly across the sky, their edges shining pale blue.

Mitya stood at the edge of the deck, leaning on the handrail, staring in silence toward the shore.

"What have you been thinking about for so long?" Dima asked.

"The same thing," said Mitya. "What's happening to me."

"You're traveling across the sea in a launch, watching the shore."

"No," said Mitya. "Not right this moment. But what's happening to my life in general. It's strange—haven't you ever noticed how easy it is to tell someone else how they should live and what they should do? I could explain it all to anyone,

I'd even show them which lights they should fly toward. But when you need to do the same thing for yourself, you just can't find a single source of light."

"I don't see what the problem is," said Dima. "See how many lights there are out there. Choose any one you like and fly as hard as you can."

"That's the point," said Mitya. "There are two personalities inside me, and I can't tell them apart. I don't know which is the real me, and I can't tell when they change places, because both seem to want to fly toward the light, but by different routes. And they suggest doing different things."

"Who do they suggest them to?"

"To me."

"Aha," said Dima. "So now there are three of you?"

"Why three?"

"The first one, the second one, and the one they make their suggestions to."

"You're playing with words. I can put it another way. When I'm trying to reach a decision, I constantly come across someone in myself who has made exactly the opposite decision, and he's the one who does everything."

"What about you?"

"What about me? As soon as he appears, I become him."

"So he is you?"

"But I wanted to do just the opposite."

Mitya said nothing else for quite a while.

"The two of them divide up my time between them," he began again. "One is the real me, the absolute me, the one I regard as myself. The one who wants to fly toward the light. And the other is a temporary me, who exists only for a second. He basically wants to fly toward the light, too, but first he needs a last short period of darkness. As though to say good-bye, take a final look. The strange thing is that the me who wants to fly toward the light has my whole life, because he really *is* me, and the one who wants to fly into the darkness has only this final second, but even so . . ."

"But still you realize that you're flying into the darkness."

"Yes."

"And does it surprise you?"

"Very much."

Dima threw a crumpled candy wrapper overboard and watched the bright spot of color until it disappeared in the foamy wake from the propeller.

"A moth's entire life," he said, "is that second he wastes in taking leave of the darkness. Unfortunately, there is nothing else in the world except that second. This huge life, in which you intend eventually to turn toward the light, is really that single moment when you choose the darkness."

"Why?"

"What else can there be, apart from this very second?"

"Yesterday. Tomorrow. The day after tomorrow."

"Yesterday and tomorrow and the day after tomorrow, and even the day after that, exist only in the present second," said Dima. "Only in that moment, when you think about them. So if you want to choose the light tomorrow, and take your leave of the darkness today, you're really just choosing the darkness."

"But what if I want to stop choosing the darkness?" asked Mitya.

"Choose the light," said Dima.

"But how?"

"Simply fly toward it. Right now. There never will be any other time to do it."

Mitya looked toward the shore.

Something flashed through the air and there was a loud bang on the upper deck. Then they heard shoes scraping on the deck, and cheerful voices.

"What's happening over there?" Mitya asked, raising his head sharply.

"Mosquitoes," said Dima. "Three of them."

"At night?" asked Mitya. "And this far out at sea?"

"It's daytime for them," said Dima. "They think that the sun's shining brightly."

"What are they doing over there?"

"How should I know?" said Dima.

An immense rocky mountain appeared off the starboard side of the launch. It looked like a stone bird with its wings extended and its head bent forward, and there were two red lights flickering on its peak.

"See how much light and darkness there is all around us," said Dima. "Choose whatever you want."

"Let's say I want to choose the light. How will I know if it's the real light? The brightest light around is the moon, but you called it one of Lenin's lightbulbs."

"The genuine light is any light that you can actually reach. Even if you only just fail to get there, then no matter how bright the light you were flying toward, it was a mistake. The real point is not what you fly toward but who is doing the flying. But then that's the same thing."

"Yes," said Mitya, "probably. Then I choose those two red lights up there."

Dima looked up at the top of the mountain. "Not very close," he said. "But then, that doesn't matter."

"What do we do now?" asked Mitya.

"Fly."

"What, right now?"

"When else?" asked Dima.

Mitya climbed over the railing on the deck, grabbed hold of a short piece of rope tied to a flagpole, and spread his wings. A gust of wind lifted up his body, and for a moment he looked like a dark flag being raised at the stern, or a kite soaring up above it. Then he released his grip, and the launch drifted down and away from him. He saw three small figures among the inflatable life rafts cluttering the upper deck.

When Dima appeared beside him, flying quickly and inconspicuously, completely without self-indulgence, the figures on the upper deck began moving. One of them, holding a guitar case, suddenly got up from his hands and knees, ran a couple of steps, and tumbled through the air, almost falling into the sea, but just managed to fly off toward the shore, gradually picking up speed. The other two began arguing and gesticulating passionately until, just as Mitya could hardly make them out anymore, they also flew up into the air. A minute later the launch was nothing but a bright spot below him, and Mitya began looking ahead.

In front of him was a sheer rocky drop. When he was quite close to it, he had to fly almost vertically upward. After a few minutes of ascending like this, Mitya felt his perspective suddenly shift, and instead of rising up, the cliff face seemed to extend horizontally into the distance, as though he were flying low over a rocky desert, with the moonlight highlighting every projection and every crack. The red lights on the summit now looked like railroad signal lights in the distance.

A gust of wind caught him from behind, and he almost crashed into a stone ledge jutting out a long way from the side of the mountain. After that, he flew more slowly. Sometimes bushes appeared in the crevices in the cliff, looking as though they had been bent by a powerful wind. Mitya had only to remind himself that the bushes were simply reaching up as they were supposed to for the rocky plane below him to be transformed back into its real self, a wall of stone. But as soon as Mitya stopped reminding himself, the endless desert reappeared beneath, and rushing across it, stretching and twisting across the cracks, were the long black shadows of two moths. Mitya looked up. There were no red lights ahead anymore.

The moon slid behind the edge of a cloud, and the rocky plain they were flying over suddenly seemed somber and dismal. Far beyond it shone the lights of a few seaside villages, looking like stars from some other sky. Once again, Mitya looked into the dark void ahead and felt a sudden fear and a desire to turn back and fly downward.

"Listen," he said to Dima, who was flying beside him, "where are we going? The lights aren't there anymore."

"Of course they are," said Dima, "if we're flying toward them."

"What's the point of flying toward them if they've disappeared? Let's go back."

"Then we'll disappear, too. The 'we' who set off for the lights."

"Maybe they simply weren't real," said Mitya.

"Maybe," said Dima. "And maybe we weren't real."

The moon came out again, the sharp shadows of projecting rocks reappeared on the mountainside, and Mitya felt an inexplicable agitation. He shook his head and suddenly realized that for a long time he had been aware of a piercing barking sound. The barking was very loud but so subtle that instead of hearing it, he felt it in his belly. Sometimes the barking stopped and was replaced by a sound something between a howl and a whistle, which gave Mitya a slightly nauseous feeling in his throat. The timbre of the whistling was very unpleasant, and the thought came to Mitya that if the Khmer Rouge in Cambodia had made alarm clocks for export, they would ring just like that.

"Can you hear it?" he asked Dima.

"Yes," Dima said calmly.

"What is it?"

"It's a bat," said Dima.

Mitya had no time to feel frightened. A third shadow appeared, rushing up over the moonlit rocky slope and engulfing the first two. It was huge and shapeless, with blurred edges. Mitya and Dima swooped toward the cliff and hurtled down to a tiny ledge with a few small bushes growing on it. The whistling ceased.

"Don't move a muscle," said Dima. "If you heard it, then it heard you a long time ago."

"Can it hear us talking?"

"No," answered Dima. "It has a very interesting relationship with reality. First it shouts, and then it listens to the reflected sound and draws the appropriate conclusions. If we don't move at all, it might leave us in peace."

For a few minutes they stood there in silence. It was quiet

up there; the only sound was the faint murmuring of the sea below them.

"Do you remember the question I asked you?" said Dima. "About the light reflected by the sun?"

"Yes."

"In fact, neither the sun nor the light really have anything to do with it. I could ask the same question in a different way. We can take what's happening to us right now. What do you think the bat sees when the sound is reflected back from you?"

"Me, I suppose," said Mitya, gazing into the sky.

"But it made the sound itself."

"Not me, then, but its own sound," said Mitya.

The bat's barking had fallen silent, and the bat was nowhere to be seen, but Mitya could sense that it was somewhere close by, and this bothered him considerably more than any structures of logic.

"Yes," said Dima, "but the sound was reflected from you."

Mitya surveyed the sky again. Dima's calm, unhurried tone was beginning to get on his nerves.

"So it turns out that in one sense you are nothing but a sound emitted by a bat. A couplet in its song, so to speak."

A ponderous black form suddenly loomed up in front of the ledge and hurtled past, sending a gust of cold air over them. For a minute or two they heard nothing, and then they heard the same piercing barking sound in the distance. It was coming closer—the bat was obviously moving in to attack.

"If you are one of the sounds emitted by a bat, then what is the bat?"

"The thing that's just about to eat us," answered Mitya, feeling the whistling turn his legs to jelly.

He glimpsed a dark spot far off in the sky, and the whistling grew louder. In his belly Mitya sensed an inaudible melody, two octaves higher than anything he had ever heard in his life.

"Just think," said Dima. "All the bat has to do is stop whistling and you disappear. But what do you have to do to make the bat disappear?"

He pushed off from the rim of the ledge and hurtled down, headfirst. Mitya jumped after him, and the dark black mass crashed into the spot where he had just been standing, breaking the branches of the bushes.

He fell out of control for several yards, then braked and flew rapidly along the slope, almost snagging his wings on it. Dima had disappeared.

Behind him, he heard the sickening whistling sound. He glanced around and saw a dark shadow soaring and plunging as it flew. A little farther on, he noticed a narrow crevice in the cliff and darted into it. Squeezing, he pressed himself against the rough surface of the stone and froze. For a few minutes, everything was quiet and all Mitya could hear was his own loud breathing. Then he heard the whistling again from the direction of the sea, and almost immediately the dark mass crashed into the cliff, covering the opening of the crevice, and a black clawed hand raked the air just inches away from him. Mitya caught a glimpse of a broad, gray face with pointed ears, little eyes, and a huge jaw full of teeth (for some reason, it reminded him of the radiator on an old Chaika automobile). The bat rustled its wings over the rocks and disappeared. The feeling Mitya was left with was that a soft, fluffy government limousine driven by a half-blind driver had been trying to drive into the crevice where he was hiding.

Mitya shifted his weight to his left foot and drew his right foot back. The whistling came again, and when the black body of the bat began pressing into the entrance, Mitya kicked at it with all his strength. He hit something that gave way and heard a loud squeak. The bat disappeared. Mitya held his breath and waited, but there were no signs of life from the bat. Carefully creeping up to the exit, Mitya stuck his head out and immediately the piercing whistling began again. A webbed wing flashed in front of his eyes, and teeth clashed together just above his ear. Mitya leaped back and almost lost his balance.

A few minutes later, Mitya thought he could hear sounds made by the bat: the soft rustling of wings and the scraping of claws on stone. Perhaps the sounds were made by the wind, but Mitya was sure that the bat was still waiting for him. "So that's the way it is," he thought. "As soon as you realize you live in the darkness, bats start appearing out of it . . ."

Suddenly Mitya caught a faint glimpse of hope.

"What could it be afraid of?" he thought.

The first thing that came into his mind was a cat with wings. Mitya closed his eyes and tried to imagine what it would look like. The flying cat turned out to be a creature squatting on its hind legs with large fluffy wings and a tail with something like a flyswatter on the end of it, rather like an ancient drawing of a flying lizard. Painstakingly visualizing every detail of its appearance, Mitya began whistling quietly, and an upside-down face immediately appeared in the opening of the crevice. The eyes seemed to be staring doubtfully. Mitya whistled louder, and imagined the flying cat opening its jaws and pouncing. The face in the opening disappeared, and Mitya heard the beat of swiftly retreating wings.

Mitya stuck two fingers into his mouth and whistled as loud as he could after the dark receding spot. Then he stepped out of the crevice into the void and fell for a while before braking and turning back up.

Dima was nowhere to be seen. Mitya flew to the spot where they had parted, off to one side and much higher. Dima was not on the ledge, and Mitya flew on toward the top of the mountain. He was sure that nothing had happened to Dima, but even so, despite the euphoria of his unexpected victory, he had a feeling of foreboding. When he had been flying for only a few minutes, and the stone wall drifting past him seemed to be cast of metal, without a single fault or joint, he heard the whistling again and realized that the bat had not left him in peace at all. It had simply waited until he left his refuge and reached a place where there was nowhere to hide.

Mitya stuck two fingers into his mouth and whistled back as loud as he could, attempting once again to summon up the mental image of the black fluffy sphinx, but his whistle was pitiful and the whole idea seemed extremely stupid. He could just make out the bat in the distance, like a black rubber ball bouncing toward him over an invisible surface, and there was absolutely nowhere to hide from it. "What can I do to make it disappear?" Mitya thought feverishly. "To make me disappear, all it has to do is stop whistling . . . I am what it hears . . . To make it disappear, perhaps I should stop doing something as well? But what is it I do to make it appear?"

That was quite impossible to work out. He could understand what Dima had in mind in the metaphorical sense, but it wasn't clear at all what use all the metaphors might be when a very unmetaphorical bat was chasing you.

Mitya closed his eyes and saw a clear blue light, as though his eyes had been closed before but were now open wide in terror. For the first time he noticed what had always been there in front of him, but so much closer than everything else that it had been invisible. A momentary recollection flashed through his mind of a November day long ago when he could hardly drag himself through a gray park, over which low leaden clouds were drifting from the north. As he moved along, he thought that if this weather lasted a few more days the sky would sink so low it would run over people like a truck driven by a drunken driver. Then he raised his eyes to a gap in the clouds, through which he could see white clouds high up and far away, and beyond them the sky, exactly as it was in summer, so blue and pure that it was quite obvious that nothing ever happened to the sky, and that no matter what repulsive clouds might gather for the state holidays in Moscow, high above them there was always this pure, unchanging vault of blue.

It was a great surprise now to see in himself something similar, as unaffected by what was happening around it as the sky that was the same at all seasons of the year was unaffected by the clouds which scurried over the face of the earth.

"It all depends," thought Mitya, "on what side you look at

things from. Stop. Just who is it who's looking, anyway? And at whom?"

•

He opened his eyes. He was suspended in a spot of bright blue light, as though caught in the crossed beams of several searchlights. But in fact there weren't any searchlights; he himself was the source of the light. Mitya held his hands up in front of his face. They were glowing with a clear, pure blue light, and tiny silvery midges that had appeared out of nowhere so high above the sea were circling around them.

Mitya flew up, and all the time, while he was moving toward the summit, he didn't have a single thought.

The summit proved to be a small flat ledge with a few hawthorn bushes growing on it beside the tall steel shaft of a beacon. Once again he could see the two red lamps, which had been hidden by the projecting rocks. They lit up alternately, and on the earth the dark shadows of the bushes reversed direction, like the shadow of a pendulum swinging to and fro. Oddly enough, there were two folding stools beside the shaft supporting the two red lamps, and Dima was sitting on one of them.

Mitya waved to him, sat on the other stool, took a piece of paper from his pocket, and spread it out on his knees.

"Just a moment," he said in answer to Dima's attentive gaze. "Just a moment."

He wrote for a minute or so, then quickly folded the sheet of paper into an airplane, got up, walked to the edge of the cliff, and launched it. At first it nose-dived, then it soared back up and off to the right, in the direction of the tourist village.

"What did you do that for?" asked Dima.

"Nothing too serious," said Mitya. "A mystical debt owed to Marcus Aurelius."

"Ah," said Dima. "Sometimes debts have to be paid. Now tell me, what light does the sun reflect?"

Mitya stuck a cigarette in his mouth, clicked his lighter,

and a small bright blue tongue of flame appeared above it.

"Right," said Dima. "How simple everything is, isn't it?"

"Yes," said Mitya, "it's amazing."

He looked up at the lamps blinking on and off overhead. The air around the glass covers was a trembling mass of hundreds of unfamiliar insects, trying in vain to break through the thick ribbed glass to the source of the light.

"Where did the bat go?" Mitya asked.

"Where could it go? There it is, flying around."

Dima pointed to a tiny black lump soaring and plunging through the air at the edge of the illuminated area. Mitya looked, and then he glanced at his own hands: they were still bathed in an even blue glow.

"I've just realized," he said, "that we're not really moths at all. And not . . ."

"It's probably not even worth trying to express it in words," said Dima. "And anyway, nothing around you has changed just because you've understood something. The world's just the same as it was. Moths fly toward the light, flies fly toward shit, and they're all in total darkness. But now you'll be different. And you'll never forget who you really are, right?"

"Of course," replied Mitya. "There's just one thing I don't understand. Have I just turned into a firefly, or was I always one?"

INSECT MURDER

"And finally," said Arthur, looking with unconcealed pleasure at Arnold, who had stuck his head under the running tap, "you shouted loud enough for the whole station to hear, 'Are we just going to stand by and watch while American mosquitoes fuck our flies?'"

Arnold covered his face with his hands, and the water flowed down his forearms, swirled over his elbows, and splashed onto the tiles in two separate streams.

"But the most interesting thing is that the police obviously sympathized with you," said Arthur. "They even gave you back your money, and that's very unusual. Don't you remember anything at all?"

Arnold shook his head sharply.

"I did a couple of minutes ago," he said, turning off the tap and pushing his hair roughly into place. "But the last time I puked it all just went."

"You don't even remember the stuff about the Masons?" asked Arnold. "It was fascinating."

Arnold thought for a moment. "No," he said. "I don't remember."

"And the stuff about the Magadan of the spirit?"

"I don't remember that, either."

"That was the most interesting of all," said Arthur. "You told the pigs about it when they were drawing up the charges. About this special town somewhere that's really hard to get into. And they have a special art and a special science there, all just like in 1980—the final bulwark. And time is different there. For one day that goes by here, years and years go by there. A kind of Soviet Shambhala, only in reverse. But the entrance is either underground or up in the air, I didn't understand that part. And you told everyone you had connections there."

"I don't remember," said Arnold. "And anyway, that's enough. We've been through it all."

"Okay," said Arthur, "I suppose we have. Just tell me, though, what made you take the chance? You saw what happened to Sam."

"I can't really say," said Arnold. "I picked up the case, and the client was sleeping like a log. I started wondering how it would affect me. So I drank some, and then I set out, and it seemed okay. Well, I thought, Sam's a real weakling. I set off to meet you, and then . . . All I remember is that Sam was sitting at a table. And who was that girl with him?"

"I don't know," said Arthur. "I couldn't understand that myself. She just appeared at the table, out of nowhere. It's hunger that makes them so quick nowadays."

Arnold stood in front of the mirror and tidied himself up as best he could, then placed a coin on the table in front of the old female attendant. They went out of the public rest rooms and set off toward the sea.

"Listen," said Arthur, "we have nothing to do till evening. Why don't we call on Archibald?"

"Is he still in the same old place?"

"I think so," said Arthur. "I pass his hut sometimes, only I never have time to drop in. But the door's always open."

A few minutes later they reached a small log cabin standing

on the grass, its open door facing the boardwalk: it was so small that it looked as if it had been taken from a children's playground. There was a sign above the door, with a red cross, a red crescent, and a large drop of blood, and above it in red were the words: *Donor Station.*

Arthur pushed the door and entered. Arnold smoothed down his hair one last time and stepped in after him.

It was dark inside. Opposite the door was a low counter with several medicinal-looking jars and an electrical sterilizer for syringes. Behind the counter, against the wall, was a dust-covered contraption made of glass vessels joined by orange rubber tubes. Arnold knew this mound of flasks and retorts was absolutely no good for anything, nothing but a piece of stage scenery, but even so he felt as though he were in a hospital. There was no one behind the counter, but there was a dusty notice on the wall, drawn in ballpoint pen with a stencil:

BROTHERS AND SISTERS!
Help others with your blood!
Science has demonstrated that giving blood regularly enhances sexual performance and increases the donor's lifespan. It is your moral, civic, and religious duty to give!
After the donation is taken, each donor receives a free bar of Finishing Line chocolate. Regular donors are awarded an honorary-donor badge and certificate

There was no one at all in the hut, but the door at the back was half open. Arnold walked around the counter and glanced outside into a small green oasis, a stretch of lawn fenced off on all sides by thick bushes. In the center of the patch of green stood a short, rotund man wearing a doctor's coat and a cap. He was holding a plastic helicopter set on a stick with a pull cord, and just as Arnold looked through the doorway, he jerked on the cord with all his might.

The helicopter's rotor blades were transformed into a transparent disk of color and the toy soared up into the air. The man threw his head back, gave a gentle, happy laugh, and jumped up and down on the spot several times in delight. The helicopter hovered motionless for a moment, then began to fall to one side and disappeared behind the bushes. The man rushed toward the door and almost collided with Arnold. He stopped and gawped.

"Arnold!" he said, dropping the stick and cord.

"Hello there, old mate," said Arthur, emerging from the doorway.

"Hi, guys," said Archibald, looking his visitors up and down in confusion as they shook hands. "Great you came. I was beginning to think you'd gone away. How're things? What are you up to nowadays?"

"Things are just great," said Arthur. "We're setting up a joint venture with an American. How about you?"

"Everything's just the same with me," said Archibald. "Here, I won't be a moment. Take a seat."

He dashed in the door and appeared a minute later with a large retort full of dark red liquid and three glasses. He set the glasses on the grass, filled them to the brim, and raised his own.

"Whose is it?" inquired Arthur.

"It's a cocktail," answered Archibald. "Turkmenian second group and Moscow region engineer with negative rhesus factor. Cheers!"

He took a large swallow. Arthur and Arnold took a mouthful each.

"Agh, what dreck!" said Arthur with a grimace. "I'm sorry, but how can you drink it like that, with preservatives?"

"Can't be helped," said Archibald with a shrug. "Otherwise, it curdles in a day."

"Is this how you live? When was the last time you drank fresh blood?"

"Yesterday," said Archibald. "Fifty grams. When there are plenty of clients, I treat myself."

"From a glass!" snorted Arthur. "What kind of mosquito are you? What would your father say if he could see you?"

"As for what kind of mosquito I am," Archibald said apologetically, "you mustn't forget my mother was a ladybug and my father was a cockroach. I've no idea what I am."

"And how does it feel not knowing who you are?"

Archibald drained down his portion of blood and thoughtfully waved the empty glass to and fro.

"Not knowing who I am?" he repeated. "I don't know. I think I like it. It makes for a quiet life. Of course, when I was young, I didn't think I would end up like this. I always thought I was going to step through a doorway into something astonishing, something new, and with just a little bit more . . ." He stopped, fumbling for a word, and twiddled his fingers in the air, as though trying to show them what he had once wanted to devote his short life span to. "Just a little more time and I would step through that door. But the door turned out to be . . ."

He nodded toward the door into the hut.

"When was the last time you flew?" asked Arthur.

"I can't even remember. You're filling my head with sad thoughts. What's the point, guys?"

"In your heart you haven't given up yet," said Arthur. "I knew it as soon as I saw the toy helicopter."

"Maybe I haven't," said Archibald. He splashed some blood from the retort into his glass. "Like some?"

Arthur glanced inquiringly at Arnold, who shook his head.

"Listen," said Arthur, "I've got a suggestion. You lock up your hut for a couple of hours and we'll fly down to the beach. We'll drink some real blood and get some fresh air. Okay?"

"Out of the question," said Archibald. "I couldn't fly a hundred feet any more."

"Stop that," said Arnold. "You'll get there. You've lost your appetite for life. If you want to get it back, you have to bite off a bit and chew it. If you don't fly now, what's ever going to make you do it?"

"You'll just curl up and die here with all your syringes and tubes," said Arthur. "Begging your pardon, of course."

"Maybe I've died already," said Archibald, peering sullenly at his friends.

"Let's check," said Arthur, refusing to give up. "If you fly, you're alive. If you stay here, you're dead."

"Come on," said Arnold. "We'll watch out for you."

The blood he had drunk was beginning to affect Archibald. He laughed bitterly, stood up, and swayed unsteadily.

"Let me just lock the door," he said with a slight Central Asian accent and disappeared into the hut.

A moment later he stuck his head out the door, waved a long sharp knife at Arthur and Arnold, smiled evilly, and disappeared back behind the door.

Arnold leaned over to Arthur and whispered: "We should never have started all this. Maybe we should just leave, or we might really get stuck with him."

"Too late," Arthur whispered back.

It really was too late. Archibald emerged from his house: he'd changed his clothes, and now he was wearing heavy hiking boots, an army shirt, and jeans held up by an officer's belt. He was carrying a guitar case into the bargain, which made him look like an aging Moscow engineer on his way to a hootenanny.

Arthur and Arnold exchanged glances.

"You know," said Arnold, "we didn't mean you had to drop everything and go flying this very minute. We just meant that at least every now and then . . ."

"Are we going flying or not?" Archibald asked scornfully.

"We are, we are," said Arthur, paying no attention to Arnold's furious glances.

He went down on all fours, peered at Archibald, blew out his cheeks, began making quiet whirring noises, put one hand to his chest, and then flung it out sharply to the side, as though he was pulling on a string. The flaps of his jacket shuddered into movement and were transformed into a whirling circle of transparent color as he slowly rose several feet into the air, clearly parodying the flight of the little plastic helicopter.

Archibald turned red in the face, soared up into the air with amazing ease, and hovered opposite his opponent. Arthur went on playing the fool. He made whirring noises, pulled on his invisible string, and swayed from side to side as Archibald watched him somberly. Arnold flew over to Archibald, glanced at him, and turned his head away in pity. Archibald's proboscis was bent downward and it looked crumpled.

"Where to?" asked Archibald.

"Let's fly over the beach," said Arthur, "then take our bearings."

•

The boardwalk appeared below them. Then came the plank roofs of the cabanas and the open beach, with hundreds of motionless half-naked bodies lying on it. The smell of the sea mingled with a multitude of other beach smells. The beachgoers were lying so close together it was like a gang shower, and neither Arthur nor Arnold felt the slightest desire to land.

"Why don't we go to the nature preserve?" suggested Arthur, gesturing with his proboscis toward the cliff face in the distance. "There's not usually such a crowd there."

"The warden wouldn't leave us in peace," said Arnold.

"He's never there."

"But will we find a client?"

"There are always one or two," said Arthur, putting his head down and flying in front, trying not to go too fast, but not so slow that Archibald would realize they were making it easy for him.

The seashore ran in a long concave arc, but the three

friends were flying in a straight line over the sea. At first Archibald really enjoyed flying, and was annoyed with himself for neglecting such a pleasure for so many years, but when fatigue dispelled the rush of blood to his head and he looked down, he was horrified.

Below the legs pressed against his belly and the guitar which they were clutching like a missile slung under the belly of a B-52, there lay the open sea. It was a long way beneath him, and the waves on its surface appeared quite motionless. The shore was so far away that Arnold realized that if he fell now he'd never make it by swimming. He was terrified, and he rolled his eyes up to heaven.

Arthur and Arnold were in high spirits, exchanging asides about the weather, and they seemed to have forgotten about Archibald. They were flying farther and farther away from the shore, and Archibald went into a panic: his fear made him flap his wings faster than necessary. At first he thought he could make it to the nature preserve after all, and he almost relaxed, having decided never again to get himself into an adventure like this, when suddenly he felt a powerful blow to his face and chest.

Archibald screwed up his stinging eyes and raised one foot to wipe them. When he looked at it, the entire foot was covered with coarse tobacco. There was tobacco in his eyes and mouth, and stuck in his hair, but Archibald had no time to wonder where so much tobacco had come from at such an altitude—his guitar had suddenly become extremely heavy, and he felt that his wings would fail in another couple of feet.

"Hey, guys," he called to Arthur and Arnold. Realizing they couldn't hear him, he buzzed as loud as he could. "Guys!"

They turned around and understood immediately what the problem was.

"Can you make it to shore?" asked Arthur, hurrying back to him.

"No," panted Archibald. "I'm going to fall any second."

In front of Archibald's eyes, everything merged into a sense-less blur; the last thing he saw was a tiny white boat against a dark blue background.

"That's right, Arnold, let's take him . . . Like we're landing on an aircraft carrier. Can you make it to the deck?"

Archibald heard these last words from some other dimension: his world no longer had any height, or deck, or any need to make it anywhere. But the voices became louder and more insistent, and someone was shaking him hard by the shoulder, and then he had to open his eyes. Arthur and Arnold were bending over him.

"Archibald," said Arthur, "can you hear me?"

Archibald raised himself up on his elbows without speaking. He was lying on the upper deck of a launch, surrounded by inflatable orange life rafts. Their color reminded him of the dusty rubber tubes hanging on the wall of his home, and he immediately felt calmer. The launch was swaying gently. He could hear the shouts of passengers on the lower deck above the noise of the engines.

"You gave us a good scare," said Arnold. "We only just managed to catch you in the nick of time. What's wrong with you, vertigo?"

"Something like that," Archibald said.

"It's dangerous to fly any lower over the sea," said Arthur. "Seagulls."

He nodded in the direction of the stern, where several white birds hung motionless in the air. They were flying at exactly the same speed as the launch, but without flapping their wings, as though they were drawn behind it on invisible threads. From time to time, someone on the deck threw a crust into the water, and then one of the birds would pivot its wings very slightly, drift back and away from them, and turn into a white spot bobbing on the water, while its place above the stern was taken by another.

Suddenly two dark shadows with broad wings soared up

from the stern and off into the sky. It happened so quickly that neither Arnold nor Arthur noticed anything.

"Beautiful," said Archibald, and tried to get up.

"Bend down," commanded Arthur. "They'll see you from the cabin."

Archibald turned around a few times and finally settled on his hands and knees, with his face toward the white foamy wake.

"God!" he said. "What a life I've been living. It's all wrong!"

"Calm down," ordered Arthur. "Us, too. But don't get hysterical about it."

"The sea," said Archibald, slowly and distinctly. "A launch sailing across it. Seagulls. And it's all right here. And I . . . He went out on the deck, and there was no deck . . ."

In the distance, close by the mountain, several flat rocks rose up out of the water. Archibald caught a glimpse of two naked bodies lying on one of them, and then they disappeared behind the cliff face. Archibald gave an inarticulate groan, as though all the self-hatred that had been building up in his heart for so long, all the contempt for his flabby body and his senseless life, had suddenly surged to the surface, and before his friends could do anything to stop him, he had grabbed the guitar and flung himself into the air.

His field of awareness narrowed into something like a rocket's targeting system, registering nothing but the flat rock with two bodies lying on it, which came closer and closer, filling up the whole of space. Then his new target became the woman's leg that was hurtling toward him, and Archibald could feel his proboscis straightening up and swelling with a long-forgotten strength. He buzzed loudly in his happiness and thrust himself at full speed toward the yielding skin, thinking how Arthur and Arnold . . .

But then some terrible weight came crashing down out of the sky, something final and unambiguous—and suddenly there was no need to think, nothing to think about, and no one to do the thinking.

•

"I didn't mean to," Natasha repeated, with her eyes red from crying, pressing her crumpled dress to her naked breasts. "I didn't mean to! I didn't even notice!"

"Nobody's accusing anybody," Arthur said dryly. He was wet. "It's simply an accident, a very unfortunate accident."

Sam put his arms around Natasha and turned her away, so that she no longer had to look at the thing that once walked the earth, took joy in life, sucked blood, and called itself Archibald. Now it was a tangled lump of bloody meat, covered in places with fabric, with the cracked neck of a guitar protruding from its middle: no arms, no legs, and no head were visible.

"We were riding on the launch," said Arnold, "and suddenly out of the blue he took off. And so fast we couldn't overtake him. We shouted to you, we kept shouting. But when we got here . . . You didn't even notice anything. He was dragged back out to sea. It took us half an hour to find him."

"If anyone's to blame," said Arthur, "we are. He didn't want to fly at first, as though he sensed something. But then he agreed. He probably just decided to die like a mosquito."

"Perhaps," said Arnold. "What was that he said about the deck?"

"It's from an old song about the cruiser *Varangian*," said Arthur. "He went out on deck, and there was no deck. His sight blurred, and he saw a blinding light. He fell, and his heart beat no longer . . ."

"Yes," said Arnold, "it comes to us all sometime."

Something light and sharp pricked his cheek, and in a reflex action he caught at a small airplane made out of a sheet of paper covered with writing. Arnold looked up at the wall of rock which rose almost sheer above him for several hundred feet. He unfolded the airplane (the lines of its folds spread out from the upper edge like rays of light, but their intersection was beyond the edge of the paper) and read the following:

IN MEMORY OF MARCUS AURELIUS

A strictly balanced meter and rhythm
Is never produced by an attitude of sober calm.
Verse should be written in a burst of great enthusiasm
Like a People's Artist hacking out some crude triangular charm.

Anguish cleanses and vile autumnal happiness is only for fools,
In any case, it's clear that any failure or success
Is like a dream of yourself and three firemen comparing tools,
In which you find you have a little bit more or less.

Sometimes you wake up at night at about ten to three,
Gaze out of the window at the light of what they call the moon,
Recall the world is a hallucination of police informer Nickleby,
Who in turn is the hallucination of some drunken loon.

It's a good thing, too, to have your run-ins with the madmen
As they pursue you, waving their razors and drinking beer.
You run away from one, then another, then a third one,
And don't have a moment to feel your loneliness and fear.

It would be good just to lie low until the summer,
And keep your head well down out of sight,
Making sure the KGB doesn't catch the slightest glimmer
Of your bright circle of the universe's all-pervading light.

The final quatrain had been added in vigorous slanting handwriting, obviously in haste. "KGB" had been crossed out, and "AFB" written in above it, and then also crossed out. Beside it were the letters "FSK," also erased, and replaced again finally by the more permanent "KGB."

THE BLACK RIDER

Maxim closed the gate behind him. The wolfhound belonging to the master of the house walked slowly toward him from behind the dog roses, thoughtful and quiet, with sad red eyes. Strands of saliva hung from its mouth, gleaming like diamond pendants and making the dog look like some enchanted princess. The wolfhound glanced mistrustfully at Maxim's red forage cap with the yellow tassel and the heavy inscription in ballpoint pen, *Viva il Duce Mussolini*, and he had his mouth open, ready to bark when he saw the officer's boots that Maxim had polished painstakingly that morning, and that confused him.

"*Banzai!*" called a woman in a dressing gown, with her hair hanging loose, as she emerged from the bushes after the dog. "*Banzai!*"

"*Banzai!*" Maxim shouted joyfully in reply, but what he had taken for an unexpected (and therefore all the more wonderful) gesture of the spirit proved to be a misunderstanding. The woman was not greeting him, as he thought for a moment, but simply calling the dog. Maxim coughed loudly into his hand and thought how he was always wrong about people, always thinking too well of them.

"I'm sorry," he said in a well-trained baritone. "Is Nikita home?"

The woman of the house dragged the dog away without answering. Maxim knocked gently at a window covered on the inside with aluminum foil. A small square of blackness opened up in the foil, and an eye with an extremely wide pupil peered out. Then the square was closed again, and there was the squeaking of a small table being moved aside behind the door. In the crack there appeared Nikita's pale face, twined around with a sparse, crinkly beard. Nikita first looked behind Maxim, and only when he was sure there was nobody and nothing else outside the door did he take off the safety chain.

"Come in," he said.

Maxim went in. While Nikita was locking the door and propping the table against it, Maxim looked around. The interior hadn't changed at all, except for a new display stand Nikita had picked up somewhere, *Imperialism's Means of Aerial Aggression*, covered with big black-and-white photographs of airplanes. It was leaning against an old pile of compressed trash, in which Maxim could distinguish only a few old canvas cots. The mattress on which Nikita slept was covered with several blankets, and spread on top of them was a newspaper, with a huge pile of weed on it. From its dark green color with a reddish tinge Maxim identified it as badly overdried northwestern Chuiskaya valley hash from the late spring harvest of the previous year. It looked like a respectable pile, about seven glasses and seven boxes of matches, and Maxim suddenly felt a simple and calm joy in existence, which gradually crystallized as a sense of confidence, not only for the next day but for at least the next two weeks. Beside the newspaper lay a large magnifying glass, a sheet of paper on which there were several green spots, and Nikita's favorite book, *Spacers*, open at a page in the middle.

"You got any *papyrosi*?" asked Nikita.

Maxim nodded and took a pack of Kazbek out of his pocket.

"Blow them yourself," said Nikita, picking up the magnifying glass and bending down over the sheet of paper.

Maxim squatted down beside the newspaper and opened the pack of Kazbek. The black silhouette of a horseman on the pack gave him an uneasy feeling, and he took out several of the cigarettes with their long cardboard tubes for tips and hid the pack away in his pocket. He took one of them, turned the end filled with tobacco toward the stand with the photographs, and blew hard into the hollow cardboard tip. The tobacco filling flew out of the paper cylinder and smashed into one of the black airplanes. Maxim read the words underneath it and saw he'd hit a B-52 Stratofortress bomber, complete with a "hound dog" missile slung under its fuselage.

"The target has been destroyed," he whispered, then took the empty *papyrosa* in his lips, leaned over the pile of weed, and began sucking it into the paper tube.

Nikita, an acknowledged master of pneumatic packing, watched Maxim's efforts with a sullen, even somewhat disgusted expression, but he made no comment. He favored a slightly different technique, which left a little tobacco in the end of the *papyrosa*; the point wasn't so much that this method kept the grass from getting into your mouth as that it was directly inherited from the sixties generation, which Nikita greatly admired, and Maxim, like all post-modernists, dismissed out of hand. When Maxim packed a joint, he simply twisted the paper close to the cardboard, and the result was a "tobacco-free joint."

Rolling three joints, Maxim handed one to Nikita, put one in his pocket, and struck a match to light the third.

"Good plant material," he said after a couple of drags. "But still not as good as the Marshall Plant. More like the Secret Plant of World Zionism, eh?"

"I don't think so," Nikita said. "More like Lenin's Plant for an Armed Uprising."

"Ah, yes," said Maxim, rising to the occasion. "Like the stuff he grew in Germany and handed out to the soldiers?"

"Yeah. And then there was the State Electrification Plant."

"The stuff we smoked last week? I didn't like that much. It gave me these yellow circles in front of my eyes."

"And then there was Lenin's Cooperative Plant," muttered Nikita, "the Industrialization Plant, and the Plant for Building Socialism in a Single Country."

"When was 'then,' when you got the stuff or when Lenin was handing it out?"

"Yes," said Nikita.

"But there was no Marshall Plant then," concluded Nikita. Marshall Plant was the name for a quite remarkable kind of weed from the Far East, which the previous summer had skirted the outer periphery of Nikita's world, out where the complicated criminal deals began, and where they preferred to sell weed for bullets rather than money. Only a very little Marshall Plant actually came through, but it had made such an impression that every new delivery was inevitably compared with it.

When he finished his joint, Nikita picked up the magnifying glass and leaned over the sheet of paper with the scattered green dots.

"What's that you're looking at?" asked Maxim.

"Hemp bugs," said Nikita.

"What're hemp bugs?"

"Never seen them?" Nikita asked in a melancholy voice. "Take a look."

Maxim moved closer to the sheet of paper. There were pieces of dry hemp on it, all about the same size, an eighth of an inch long, and all consisting of a section of leaf and a short length of stem, which made them all the same triangular shape. Maxim made a quick guess as to how long it must have taken Nikita to sift through a whole pile of weed to collect these bits, and he gave his friend a glance of admiration.

"You're putting me on," he said. "Don't tell me these are bugs!"

"That's what I thought at first," said Nikita. "But take a look through the magnifying glass."

Maxim took the glass and bent over the paper. At first he didn't notice anything unusual in the magnified fragments of leaf, but then he saw they had strange symmetrical striped markings, which he suddenly recognized as legs pressed tight against bellies. Then there was an incredible transformation, the way it happens with those puzzles where you recognize a drawing of something in a chaotic tangle of lines. The entire sheet of paper, which before had been covered with hemp debris, was now scattered with small flat brownish-green insects with oblong heads, hard triangular bodies—the bugs obviously still had rudimentary wings, he could even see the line dividing them—and legs pressed against their bodies.

"Are they dead," asked Maxim, "or sleeping?"

"No," answered Nikita, "they're just pretending. If you don't watch them for a long time, they start crawling around."

"I'd never have guessed," muttered Maxim. "Whoa, they're moving now. When did you notice them?"

"Yesterday," said Nikita.

"Yourself?"

"Uh-uh," said Nikita. "Someone showed me. I didn't know about them either."

"Are there many of them in the weed?"

"Lots," said Nikita. "Twenty of them in every box. At the very least."

"Then why didn't we notice them before?" asked Maxim.

"They're very cunning. And they pretend to be weeds. But they give this sign. A day before the pigs arrive, they abandon the stash, just like rats leaving a sinking ship. So people who are smart take a bunch of weed and put it on top of a cupboard and cover it with a big gallon jug. And if the bugs crawl out and up onto the walls of the jar, then it's time to gather up all your weed and take it to some other stash."

"You mean to say," said Maxim, "they're in every joint?"

"Practically. Didn't you ever notice something crackling sometimes when you're smoking? And the smell changes?"

"But that's the seeds," said Maxim.

"That's what I used to think, too," said Nikita. "But yesterday I packed a joint just with seeds. Nothing of the sort."

"You mean it's . . ."

"Yes," said Nikita. "It's them."

The joint in Maxim's hand crackled and gave out a long stream of smoke, as if a microscopic volcano had erupted inside. Maxim glanced at it in fright and then looked at Nikita.

"Now you see," said Nikita.

"But that happens three or four times with every joint," Maxim said, turning pale.

"That's what I'm telling you."

Nikita sat on the floor and began putting on his shoes.

"What're you doing that for?" asked Maxim.

"I've just got this urge to get out of here," explained Nikita. "You got a watch?"

"No."

"Then turn on the radio. They'll tell us what time it is. I've got to be at the market at three."

Maxim reached out to the old radio and clicked the switch. They were in the middle of the news.

"Speaking at a session of the United Nations," said a xylophonic female voice, "King Hussein of Jordan said that he thought the American plant for a Middle East settlement was ineffective. He announced that the Arab nations had their own plant, with which the international community should become more familiar. And now a few words about events here at home. There are reports from the Kuzbas that at the Novoktamatorsky Metallurgical Plant the seventh blast furnace since the beginning of the five-year plant has been lit. For our listeners' information, one furnace is equal to ten glasses, or a hundred matchboxes, or a thousand joints."

Nikita bent down and switched off the radio.

"No time to wait," he said. "We'll ask someone out on the street."

"A thousand joints," Maxim repeated in a dreamy voice, opening his eyes wide. "Hey, did you hear what they were saying on the radio?"

"Sure," answered Nikita. "What of it?"

"And you're not a bit surprised?"

"Nah."

"You're too cool," Maxim said, laughing. "A real dope-head. Didn't you notice anything at all?"

"What should I have noticed?"

"About the five-year plant—there aren't any more five-year plants."

"There may not be any more five-year plants," said Nikita, "but there's still five-year plant material. They've dried enough for five years in advance."

"Ah-ah!" said Maxim, catching on.

"Let's go quick," said Nikita, glancing out the window, "while there's no one around outside. Shall we take the other joint with us?"

"Sure," said Maxim, sticking the *papyrosa* into his pocket.

Nikita stopped at the door. "Stop," he said. "That's no good."

"What's no good?"

"You look way too fishy, that's what. Turn your cap around."

Maxim obediently took off his cap and then put it back on with the tassel in the front. That was good enough for Nikita, and he opened the door.

Outside, it was windy and cool; it had rained not long before, but the pavement was already dry. Maxim and Nikita went out on the road and set off uphill toward a gleaming gateway which was formed by a pipe from the heating plant rising up over the road in the form of a square arch.

"Listen," said Nikita, "let's not go that way."

"Why not?"

"Look at that," said Nikita, pointing toward the arch. "Looks like a gallows, eh?"

Maxim looked ahead. "Nonsense," he said. "You're just tripping. Let's go."

But after what Nikita had said, they both seemed afraid of walking under the pipe, and they clambered over it a few paces to the right of the arch, getting their pants legs wet from the damp grass and mud smeared all over their shoes. Nikita looked down at Maxim's feet.

"Why are you wearing cavalry boots?" he asked. "It's hot."

"I'm getting into my part," answered Maxim.

"What part?"

"Gaev. We're doing *The Cherry Orchard*."

"Have you got it?"

"Almost. There's just a few things not clear yet about the climax. I can't quite see it all yet."

"What's a climax?" asked Nikita.

"The climax is the point that illuminates the entire role. For Gaev, it's the place where he says they've found him a job in a bank. Everyone else is standing there with shears in their hands, and Gaev looks them over slowly and says, 'I'm going to work in the bank.' Then someone behind him sticks an aquarium over his head, and he drops his bamboo sword."

"What's the bamboo sword for?"

"Because he's playing billiards," Maxim explained.

"And the aquarium?" asked Nikita.

"It's obvious," answered Maxim. "Post-modernism. De Chirico. Come and watch if you like."

"No, I'm not going to come," said Nikita. "That basement of yours stinks of sealing wax, and I don't like post-modernism. It's the art of Soviet night watchmen."

"What do you mean?"

"They just got bored of sitting there all the time, so they thought up post-modernism. Just listen to the word."

"Stop being such a jerk, Nikita," said Maxim. "You worked as a janitor, too, didn't you?"

On their left they caught a glimpse of the sea through a gap in the hills, but the road turned to the right and the sea disappeared. There was no one ahead of them. Maxim reached into his pocket, took out the joint, and lit it.

"Sure I did," said Nikita, taking the smoking *papyrosa*, "and I never caused anybody any hassle. But even before you settled into that basement you were a parasite. Remember the time I asked to swap a picture for three matchboxes?"

"What picture?" Maxim asked in an unnatural voice.

"As if you don't remember: *Death by Harpoon Gun in the Garden of the Golden Masks*," said Nikita. "What did you do? You cut out a triangle in the middle and wrote in 'prick.' "

"Come on, man," Maxim retorted with cold dignity. "What's all the fuss about? That's all water under the bridge. I was a conceptual artist then, and that was a happening."

Nikita took a deep pull of smoke and coughed.

"You're a pile of shit," he said when he got his breath back, "and not a conceptual artist. You just don't know how to do anything else except cut out triangles and write 'prick,' and think up fancy titles for yourself. You've even cut a triangle out of *The Cherry Orchard* and written 'prick' on it. All this post-modernism is nothing but a pile of triangles and pricks."

"I killed the conceptual artist in myself long ago," Maxim said in a conciliatory tone.

"I was wondering what that stench coming out of your mouth was."

Maxim stopped and was about to open his mouth to speak, when he remembered that he wanted to borrow some weed from Nikita and he restrained himself. Nikita always behaved like this when he felt someone was about to ask him for weed.

"You're just like my local militia sergeant, Nikita," Maxim said quietly. "He used to explain life to me, too. 'Maxim,' he used to say, 'you don't want to take a real job in a factory, and so you go thinking up all kinds of nonsense.' "

"He was right. The only difference between you and that sergeant is that when he puts on his boots he doesn't realize it's an aesthetic statement."

"And just who are you?" said Maxim, his self-control failing. "Are you telling me you're not a post-modernist? You're exactly the same kind of shit."

But Nikita had got hold of himself, and his eyes were once again veiled with languid melancholy.

"It was a good picture, too," said Maxim. "*Death by Harpoon Gun*. Which of your periods was it from? Astrakhan?"

"Nah," answered Nikita. "Kirghizian."

"I'm sure it was the Astrakhan period," said Maxim.

"Nah," said Nikita. "The Astrakhan period was *Non-Humanoid Prisoners at the Headquarters of the Kiev Military District*. I had a long Kirghizian period, then a short Astrakhan one, and another Kirghizian one. I'll never forgive Gorbachev for losing Central Asia. He wrecked a great country."

"You think he meant to?" Maxim asked, trying to steer the conversation as far away as possible from this dangerous topic. "He just didn't have any clear plant of action."

Nikita dropped the conversation. The highway they were walking along was taking them farther and farther away from the sea. They were surrounded by bare hills, and Maxim thought that if it started raining again, they'd have nowhere to take shelter. He felt a chill run through him.

"Let's go back," he said. "Hey, leave me the butt!"

Nikita took a final drag and handed the butt to Maxim.

"Why go back?" he said. "We'll turn off here. We can go straight through."

A narrow paved road led off the highway. Beside it ran a long wooden fence, and behind that they could see the unfinished buildings of a health spa and a pair of cranes. Maxim thought in alarm that there might be dogs along the road, but when Nikita turned off the highway, he followed him without saying anything.

Suddenly an unpleasant thought came to him. "Listen, Nikita, what was that you were saying about the glass jar and the hemp bugs?"

"Ah. They stick this stash of weed under a jar and watch it. If the bugs creep out, it means there's going to be a raid."

The *papyrosa* in Maxim's hand gave a crack and released a long thin stream of smoke, like the exhaust of a rocket. Maxim shuddered.

"Tell me," he said, "why did we creep out, anyway?"

"I got this urge," said Nikita. "I just thought, what if the pigs suddenly turn up?"

"I see," said Maxim, looking round. "Let's move it."

He looked so pale that Nikita was frightened when he glanced at him, and he began taking longer strides.

"What's the hurry?" he asked.

"Haven't you got it yet?" said Maxim. "They're coming for us now."

It suddenly hit Nikita. He started walking even faster, looked around, and saw a yellow police jeep with a blue stripe along its side drawing up at the road junction.

"Stop," said Nikita, gazing crazily at Maxim. "We won't get away like that. They're driving."

"What do you suggest?"

"Let's lie down by the road and pretend to be dead. They'll go past, like they haven't seen us. What the fuck do they want extra work for?"

"You're out of your skull," said Maxim. "We've got to hide."

"Where can we hide around here?"

"In the dump," said Maxim.

Just to the left of the road there was a huge dump—or not so much a dump as a site littered randomly with every possible kind of garbage. It was used for storing building materials—cement slabs, blocks and pipes of all shapes and sizes—but there was more garbage on it than anything else. Maxim looked around and saw the jeep had turned off the highway onto the road he and Nikita were walking along.

"Run for it," whispered Maxim, dashing into the crevice between two rows of big slabs. Nikita ran after him. They heard the motor growling as it grew closer, and then it stopped.

"They've gotten out of the jeep!" Maxim whined. He slipped on a wet plank, fell, jumped to his feet, dashed around another stack of slabs, and dived into an empty concrete pipe lying on some wet boards in front of a mound of empty boxes. Nikita followed him. The pipe was almost six feet in diameter, so they didn't even have to bend down. Maxim and Nikita ran all the way through it until they reached a dead end, where the walls came together in a shallow cone, with an opening at its center about the size of a human head.

"Did they see us?" asked Nikita.

"Quiet!" whispered Maxim.

"They won't hear us," said Nikita. "The acoustics are all wrong. Don't panic."

"Who's panicking?" said Maxim. "Me? Was it me who suggested pretending to be dead, like those bugs?"

Nikita said nothing and looked toward the way out—it was a bright circle fifty feet away which seemed very small. It was damp in the pipe. He turned to look at Maxim. When Maxim began thinking, his face changed, losing its usual expression of polite dignity and looking instead like a prosthetic device: there were lots of faces like that in the photographs from the U.S.S.R. Ministry of Fisheries archives which Nikita was using in his current period. The photos had found their way into Nikita's hands after complicated double and triple deals in hash.

"We'll wait half an hour," said Maxim, "and then we can go out and take a look. You still high?"

"Yeah," said Nikita.

"Strong stuff. Can I borrow a couple of matchboxes?"

Nikita nodded.

"Damn," said Maxim, knowing that once Nikita had agreed in principle he had to change the topic of conversation as quickly as possible, "I lost my cap. Probably when I slipped."

"No," said Nikita. "You took it off before that. Look in your pockets."

Maxim put his hand in his pocket and took out the pack of Kazbek *papyrosi*.

"I've just realized something," he said. "Kazbek *papyrosi* aren't really Kazbek at all."

"Why?"

"Take a look. It says Kazbek, but what's the picture?"

"Mount Kazbek."

"That's the background," said Maxim. "But what's here in the foreground? A black rider!"

"Hold it right there," said Nikita. "Delirium's setting in."

Maxim wanted to say something, but Nikita held up his finger.

"Quiet," he whispered.

They heard voices outside. Then there was silence for a few minutes, until Maxim heard a rhythmic tapping, like the sound of someone drumming his fingers on a table. The sound came closer, and they realized it was a horse's hooves. They beat a tattoo several times around the pipe and then disappeared.

"Listen," said Maxim, getting up from the floor, "there was no need to panic. Why get so worked up? We don't have any more weed on us anyway. Let's get out of here, all right?"

"Let's go," Nikita agreed, and he got up, too.

Suddenly there was a strong gust of wind along the pipe. At first Maxim thought it was just a draft, but before he could take a step the wind knocked him down and dragged him back. Nikita managed to keep his balance and walk on for a few paces, leaning forward, but the current of air was so strong that the wooden crates piled up at the entrance to the pipe began to be sucked inside. Nikita dodged three or four of them, but the wind forced him to go down on all fours and press himself against the rough surface of the concrete. Behind him, Maxim was flattened against the end of the pipe, and the small hole above his head whistled horribly as it sucked in air. He shouted something, but Nikita couldn't understand him: the current of air carried the sound in the opposite direction. The wooden crates kept tumbling into the pipe, and one hit Nikita on his hands. He lost his grip and rolled back along the pipe toward Maxim. The wind was now so strong that the crates were flying into the pipe, shattering against the concrete walls. Nikita covered his ears with his hands and closed his eyes as he felt the pressure build up. His body was pinned down by a splintered mass of wooden slats and he could scarcely move. Then the wind stopped, as suddenly as it had started.

"Hey, Maxim!" Nikita shouted. "Are you still alive?"

"Yes. Where are you?"

"Here. Where the hell else could I be?" Nikita answered.

Maxim's back was flattened against the steep overhang of concrete, and the space around him was packed so tight with broken crates that he couldn't move a muscle. Judging from Nikita's voice, he was fairly close, maybe only ten or twelve feet away behind the debris, but Maxim couldn't see him.

"What was that?" Maxim asked.

"You mean you haven't caught on yet?" Nikita replied with malice. "We've been packed into a joint."

"I think my leg's broken," Maxim complained.

"Serves you right. How many times have I told you not to make joints without tobacco? Not that it makes any difference now, of course . . ."

"What do you mean?"

"Just think about it, Maxim."

But there was no time to think. The wind started up again, and this time it was carrying thick gusts of smoke with it. Both of them began coughing. Maxim felt a wave of scorching heat and through the gaps between the shattered slats of wood he glimpsed the red glimmer of distant flames. Then everything was enveloped in smoke, and he closed his eyes. He couldn't keep them open.

"Nikita!" he shouted.

Nikita didn't reply.

"Right," thought Maxim. "I'm at the end, and a joint is about eight drags. There've already been two. That means . . ."

Another wave of scalding heat enveloped him and he began to choke. Hot tar ran down over his hands and his face.

"Nikita!" he shouted again, trying to open his eyes.

A purple glow shone through the smoke, very close, and from the spot where he had heard Nikita's voice there was a sudden deafening crack. With a struggle Maxim managed to turn his head away from the hole, which had sucked out all the smoke, and took a breath of air.

"And if the joint is short," he thought in horror, "you can smoke it in five drags . . . Oh God! Can you hear me?"

He tried to cross himself, but he couldn't free his hand from under the splintered crates.

"God, what are you punishing me for?" he choked out.

A voice at once frightening and kindly spoke from the hole which had sucked in all the smoke.

"Surely you do not think that I wish you any harm?"

"No!" Maxim shouted, huddling against the concrete in an attempt to escape the searing heat. "No, I don't! Oh God, forgive me!"

"You have not done anything wrong," the voice intoned. "Think about something else."

FLIGHT OVER THE

NEST OF THE ENEMY

The rain drummed heavily on the roof of the bus shelter. Natasha sat on the narrow yellow bench, huddled into the cold angle of glass, and cried. Sam sat beside her and shuddered when water splashed them from the road.

"Natasha." He called her name and tried to pull her hands away from her face.

"Sam," said Natasha, "don't look at me. My eyes are all swollen."

"You must calm down," said Sam. "Take some medicine or something . . ."

He thrust two fingers into the breast pocket of his shirt, drew out a long *papyrosa* with the paper twisted at the end into the form of an arrowhead, looked at it doubtfully, and stuck it in his mouth. He lit up, took a couple of pulls on the joint, and then tapped Natasha on the shoulder.

"Here, try this."

Natasha peeped out from behind her hands. "What is it?" she asked.

"Marijuana," said Sam.

"Where did you get it?"

"You won't believe me," said Sam. "I was walking along the boardwalk this morning, before there was anyone around, and I heard hoofbeats. I turned around to look, and there was a horseman dressed all in black, wearing a long heavy cloak, riding toward me. His horse reared up and he held out this cigarette, so I took it. And then the horse neighed so loud . . ."

"What then?" asked Natasha.

"He galloped off."

"That's very strange."

"I think it's some ancient Tatar custom," said Sam. "I read about something like it in Herodotus, back in college."

"Won't it make me ill?" asked Natasha.

"It'll make you feel good," said Sam, and took another pull.

As though in confirmation of his words, the *papyrosa* in his fingers gave a loud crack and released a long thin stream of smoke. As if it was a bare electric wire, Natasha cautiously took hold of it and looked doubtfully at Sam.

"I'm afraid," she whispered. "I've never tried it before."

"Surely you do not think," Sam said tenderly, "that I wish you any harm?"

Natasha's face twisted into a grimace, and Sam realized she was about to burst into tears.

"You have not done anything wrong," he said in the same tender voice. "Think about something else."

Natasha blinked back her tears, raised the *papyrosa* to her lips, and inhaled. The *papyrosa* gave another loud crack and hissed as it released a blue stream of smoke.

"Why does it crackle like that?" asked Natasha.

"I don't know," said Sam. "What does it matter?"

Natasha threw the butt into the stream of water covered with bubbles that was flowing along the pavement between her slippers. It splashed into the water, hissed as it went out, and drifted away. The water fell over the edge of the path onto the road in a small waterfall, and when the cardboard tube tumbled over the concrete curb, Natasha lost sight of it.

"You see these bubbles, Natasha?" said Sam. "That's you and me. Insects kill each other, and most of the time they don't even know they're doing it. And no one knows what will happen to them tomorrow."

"I didn't even see him flying toward me," said Natasha. "It was just a reflex action."

"He was drunk," said Sam. "Whoever bites anyone on the thigh? Only suicide cases. It's the most sensitive spot."

He put his hand on Natasha's leg. "Does it hurt?"

Natasha looked at Sam with empty, enigmatic eyes.

"Kiss me, Sam," she said to him.

The rain was letting up. There were notices stuck on the glass walls of the bus shelter. As he pressed his lips against Natasha's, Sam saw directly in front of him a piece of paper with the words, "Fat dog for sale cheap. Phone evenings. Ask for Seryozha." The little strips of paper with the telephone number had all been torn off, and the handwriting was large, firm, and inclined to the left.

"Oh, Sam," said Natasha, "no one's ever kissed me like that before."

"Where can we go?" asked Sam.

"My mother's at home," said Natasha, "and we're not talking."

"Maybe we could go to my hotel?"

"Oh no! What would people think of me? Everybody knows everybody else around here. Better go to my place."

"What about your mother?"

"She won't see us. But she has this terrible habit of reading aloud all the time. Otherwise, she can't understand what she's reading."

"Is it far?"

"No," said Natasha. "It's very near. A few minutes at the most. Sam, I look awful, don't I?"

Sam got up, stepped out from under the shelter, and looked around.

"Let's go," he said. "The rain's stopped."

The rain had transformed the path to the resort into a torrent of mud, and the silvery Lenin rising up beside it looked like the figurehead of a ship that had been sucked down into the sticky red bog. At first Sam tried to step where the mud seemed to be less deep, but when they'd gone a few feet he began to feel as though the path was a vicious and cunning beast determined to make him as filthy as possible. He slithered across to the grass and walked there instead. His legs were soaked, but the mud on his moccasins was quickly wiped away by the grass. Natasha walked ahead, holding a slipper in each hand, maintaining her balance with astonishing grace.

"We're almost there," she said. "Go right now."

"But there's nothing but grass that way," said Sam.

"I know," said Natasha. "We live very simply, but other people are worse off. This way. Don't slip. Take my hand."

"It's okay, I can get down. Ah, damn!"

"I told you to hold my hand. Never mind, we'll wash them, and they'll be dry in an hour. Now straight ahead and then left. Bend down a bit, or you'll bang your head. This way."

"Can we have some light?"

"No, my mother will wake up. Your eyes will soon get used to it. Only don't talk too loud, or you'll wake her."

"Where is she?" Sam asked in a whisper.

"There," whispered Natasha.

Sam gradually began to make out his surroundings. They were sitting on a small divan, and beside them was a locker with a dual cassette player and a writing desk. Above the desk there was a shelf with a few books. In the corner a small white fridge was churning away softly; on its door, as if to compensate for the obvious fact that there was no meat inside, hung a poster showing Sylvester Stallone naked to the waist. About ten feet from the divan, the room was divided by a yellow curtain that reached almost to the low ceiling.

Sam took out a cigarette and clicked his lighter. Natasha tried to catch his hand, but she was too late. The flame lit up the room, and a woman moaned softly behind the curtain.

"That's it," said Natasha. "You've woken her up."

Something heavy shifted and coughed behind the curtain. Then there was a rustling of paper, and a high woman's voice began reading loudly and distinctly:

". . . But of course any insect who knows the very first thing about art no longer has the slightest doubt that virtually the only relevant aesthetic epiphenomenon of the literary process at the present time is the periodical anthology *The Triangular Prick*, of which the first number will soon be on sale. Note! The authors' opinions are not necessarily those of the publisher. Flight over the nest of the enemy. In honor of the fiftieth anniversary of the pupation of Arkady Gaidar . . ."

"Is that the politician?" whispered Sam.

"No, his grandfather. You can talk normally now," said Natasha. "She won't hear anything."

"Does she act like this often?" asked Sam.

"For days at a time. Shall we put on some music?"

"No, let's not," said Sam.

"Let me have a drag," said Natasha, sitting on Sam's knees and taking the lighted cigarette out of his fingers.

Sam put his arm around her belly and fingered the hollow of her navel through the wet green fabric.

"And so," the high voice continued monotonously behind the curtain, "it turns out that, in essence, Gaidar's prose has no reader. Adults will not read it, and children will not even notice anything, just as the English do not notice that they are reading in English. 'Farewell!' I flung at them. 'The drums are beating the campaign march. Every detachment has its own road, its own shame, its own glory.' And so we parted. The tramping of feet faded away and the field was left empty . . ."

"How can she read like that, without any light?" Sam asked softly, trying to distract Natasha's attention from the awkward pause caused by the resistance of her plastic zipper.

"I don't know," whispered Natasha. "As long as I can remember, she's done that . . . She probably remembers things off by heart."

"You see the world through the eyes of a little boy," read the voice, "not because the feelings described are primitive —they are, in fact, quite complex—but because of the infinite possibilities which the world of A *Drummer's Fate* contains. It seems to be one of the qualities of life which it is unnecessary, would even be wrong, to dwell on, this indifferent and rather sad ease with which the hero negotiates new turning points in his life. 'Now no one will know me or understand me,' I thought. 'My uncle will put me in midshipman's school, and he'll go away to Vyatka . . . Well, let him! I'll live alone and I'll do the best I can. And I won't give a damn about the past, I'll forget it, as though it never existed' . . . The universe in which the hero lives is truly beautiful: 'On the mountainside above the ravine there was a cluster of tall white buildings, looking like palaces, bright, majestic towers. As we approached they slowly unfolded to our view, half turning to gaze over each other's mighty stone shoulders, glinting with blue glass, silver, and gold' . . ."

"Natasha," said Sam, abandoning his efforts, "how does this unfasten?"

"It doesn't," Natasha said, giggling. "It's just sewn on, for decoration."

She took hold of the hem of her dress and in one swift movement pulled it up and over her head.

"Agh," she said. "Now my hair's a mess."

"But who is looking at this marvelous and ever new world?" inquired the voice behind the curtain. "Who is the observer in whose feelings we are immersed? Could it, perhaps, be the author? Or is it one of his ordinary boys, the one who a few pages later clutches the cold and reassuring barrel of a Browning in his palm? Incidentally, the theme of the child murderer is one of Gaidar's most fundamental. We recall his story *The School*, and that shot in the forest from a Mauser, which seems to resound on every page, providing the focus for the entire narrative structure. And in his latest work, *Notes from the Front*, the same theme surfaces: 'Afraid that they would not believe him, he pulled out the Komsomol membership card wrapped in oilcloth from inside his jacket . . . I looked him in the eyes. I put the cartridge clip in his hot hand . . . For sure this lad would not hide the clip away in some empty kitchen jar' . . ."

Natasha unbuttoned Sam's shirt and pressed the tender suckers on her palms against the coarse hair of his chest.

"But nowhere is this note so distinct," read the voice, more loudly, "as in *A Drummer's Fate*. Essentially, everything that takes place on the pages of this book is a prelude to the moment when the drum tattoo of gunshots is answered by a strange echo, either from the heavens above or from the very soul of this fundamentally romantic hero. 'Then I fired, once, twice, three times . . . Old Yakov suddenly stopped and staggered awkwardly. But how could I compare with the other inveterate killer, that dangerous and merciless sniper? Even as I fell, I heard the same sound, clear and pure, which neither the shots suddenly thundering through the garden nor the powerful blow from a bomb exploding close by could deafen' . . ."

Natasha's palms slid lower and encountered something reminiscent of the warm cylinder block of a racing car. Natasha realized that this was the spot from which Sam's legs grew, and she stroked it gently, then moved her hand lower until it touched the first stripe on the membranous abdomen covered with short stubble.

"Oh yeah, honey," Sam muttered. "I can feel it."

He put a hand on Natasha's cold, hard back and fondled the damp moss at the base of her trembling wings.

"It's been my dream for ages," Natasha whispered in English, repeating the optimistic intonation of the Linguaphone course, "to learn American bed whispers . . ."

"Here," responded the voice from behind the curtain, "killing is little different from, say, attempts to open the drawer of a desk using a file, or the torment of using a faulty camera. The external reality is described briefly and clearly, and the accompanying psychological process is depicted in a way which is reminiscent of the simple touching melody of a small barrel organ. Moreover, this stream of sensations, assessments, and conclusions makes no allowance for any doubts concerning the correctness of the hero's actions. Of course, he can make a mistake, do something stupid, and regret it, but he is always right, even when he is wrong. He has the natural right to act the way he does. In this sense Seryozha Scherbakhov, as the little drummer is called, attains without the slightest effort that spiritual state which Rodion Raskolnikov can only dream of. We might say that Gaidar's hero is a Raskolnikov who takes things to their conclusion, fearing nothing, because his young age and his unique experience of life make it impossible for him to realize that he could be afraid of anything. He simply cannot see the things that torment the St. Petersburg student. Raskolnikov enshrines his use of the ax in despondent and morbid introspection, but this hero cheerfully sprays bullets from his Browning after the following internal monologue: 'Stand up straight, drummer boy!' the same voice, now warm and tender, said to me. 'Stand up straight and tall! Your time has come!' Let us set aside any Freudian associations . . ."

Sam felt his proboscis straightening up under Natasha's dexterous hands, and he looked ecstatically into her eyes. A long dark tongue with a shaggy tip divided into two short hairy branches hung from her jaw. The tongue shuddered in excitement, and dark green drops of a thick secretion trickled down it.

"Eat me," whispered Natasha, tugging on the antennae protruding from beneath Sam's eyes, and he buzzed and groaned as his proboscis crunched through the green chitin of her back.

" . . . relations with Nietzscheanism were always complicated. Dostoevsky attempted to demonstrate its bankruptcy by artistic means, and he did so quite convincingly, though we must make one qualification here: he demonstrated that such a system of values was not suitable for his creation Rodion Raskolnikov. But Gaidar has created a no less convincing and no less artistically true image of the superman, that is, an image which does not contradict the author's own paradigm. Seryozha is completely amoral, and this is hardly surprising, because in all cultures any morality or any substitute for it is implanted in a child's soul by means of a special lollipop, the lollipop of beauty. Instead of the somewhat banal fascist state of A Drummer's Fate, Seryozha's blue eyes see a boundless romantic expanse, populated by tall giants engaged in a mystical battle, the nature of which is partially revealed when Seryozha asks an older superman, NKVD Major Gerchakov, what forces the adult who was killed a few days before served in: 'The man laughed. He didn't answer, but drew in the smoke from his crooked pipe, spat on the grass, and gestured lazily in the direction of the crimson setting sun.' "

Natasha pressed herself close against Sam's rapidly swelling and hardening abdomen, which had turned crimson, and pushed against it with all her six legs.

"Oh," she whispered in English, "it's getting so big and hard . . ."

"Yeah, baby," Sam answered indistinctly. "You smell good. And you sure taste good."

"And so," said the woman behind the curtain, "we have more or less clarified what Gaidar wrote. Now let us consider why he wrote it. Why should a man with a shaved head, wearing a soldier's shirt and an astrakhan hat, spend a hundred pages trying to convince someone that the world is beautiful, and that a murder committed by a child is no sin at all, because children are without sin by their very nature? Probably Yukio Mishima is the only possible choice as a soul-mate for Gaidar. We could call Mishima a Japanese Gaidar, if he had actually fired an arrow into one of the St. Sebastians of his wartime childhood. But Mishima moves from conception to action, if, that is, we can regard as action his ritual suicide after his photograph in the pose of St. Sebastian appeared in the Japanese encyclopaedia of bodybuilding, whereas Gaidar moves from action to conception, if, of course, we can regard as conception precise snapshots of the experiences of a child's soul, transferred from memory into the formaldehyde of the literary text. 'Many entries in his diary cannot be deciphered,' remarks one of the researchers. Gaidar used a special script he developed himself. Sometimes he noted that he was tormented by recurrent dreams 'with structure no. 1' or 'with structure no. 2.' And then suddenly, in plain words, like a scream erupting: 'I dreamed of the people I killed when I was a child' . . ."

The voice behind the curtain fell silent.

"Why is she stopping?" asked Sam.

"She's fallen asleep," Natasha said.

Sam gently caressed the pointed tip of her abdomen and lay back on the divan. Natasha swallowed. Sam pulled over the briefcase that was standing on the floor, opened it, took out a small glass jar, spat something red into it, screwed on the lid, and tossed it back into the case. The whole operation took only a few seconds.

"You know, Natasha," he said, "it seems to me all of us insects live for moments like this."

Natasha lowered her pale face onto Sam's dark swollen belly and closed her eyes. Tears rolled down her cheeks.

"What's wrong, honey?" Sam asked tenderly.

"Sam," said Natasha, "now you'll go away and leave me here. Have you any idea what's in store for me? Have you any idea of the way I live?"

"What do you mean?" asked Sam.

"Look," said Natasha, and showed him an oval scar on her shoulder, like the mark from a smallpox vaccination magnified several times over.

"What is it?" asked Sam.

"It's from DDT, and I've got another one on my leg from formalin."

"What, did someone try to kill you?"

"All of us," said Natasha. "They want to kill everyone who lives here."

"Who?" asked Sam.

Instead of answering, Natasha gave a loud sob.

"But there's such a thing as insect rights . . ."

"There aren't any rights," said Natasha, waving her hand dismissively. "Do you know what calcium cyanamide does? Two hundred grams in every barn? Or what it's like when they sprinkle vitriol on a cesspool and it's too late to fly away? Two of my girlfriends were killed like that, and another one, Mashenka, got dusted with lime chloride. From a helicopter. She was studying French, the silly fool . . . And you talk about the rights of insects! Have you ever heard of sulphur-carbolic mixture? One part crude sulphuric acid to three parts raw carbolic. That's all the rights we have. Nobody here has ever had any rights or ever will have any; it's just that they"— Natasha jerked her head up—"need foreign currency. For tennis rackets and tights for their wives. Sam, don't you understand? It's terrible living here."

Sam stroked Natasha's hair, glanced at the poster decorating the fridge, and remembered Sylvester Stallone, his clothing reduced by the inexorable force of circumstance to nothing but a skimpy pair of boxing trunks, on the bank of a yellowish Vietnamese river with a heavily armed slant-eyed girl. "Will you take me with you?" she asked.

"Will you take me with you?" asked Natasha.

Rambo thought for a second. "Yeah," said Rambo.

Sam thought for a second. "You see, Natasha," he began, then suddenly gave a deafening sneeze.

Behind the curtain, something large stirred and sighed. The monotonous monologue continued:

"As we close A Drummer's Fate we know what the warm and tender voice described by the author whispered to the young gun-carrying Gaidar. But why is it that this particular young marksman, whom even the Red Army command punished for his cruelty, grew up to leave us these enchanting descriptions of childhood? Is there any connection between these two things? What is the drummer's genuine fate? Who is he really? The time has come to answer these questions. Among the countless numbers of insects living in the immense expanses of our vast country, there is one which is known as the ant lion. During the first phase of its life this is a repulsive creature, something like a tail-less scorpion, which lives at the bottom of a funnel-shaped crater in the sand, eating the ants that tumble into it. Then something happens, and the monster with the fearsome claws is covered in a membranous capsule, out of which two weeks later there emerges an astoundingly beautiful dragonfly with broad wings and a narrow green abdomen. And when he flies off in the direction of the crimson setting sun, which in his previous life he could scarcely even see from the bottom of his crater, he probably does not even remember the ants that he once ate. But then . . . perhaps he dreams of them sometimes. Did it really happen to him, or . . . Major E. Fomikov. The spring of our discontent. A report from the maneuvers of the Magadan Flotilla of Assault Icebreakers . . ."

THE WELL

The blades of grass bent down under their own weight, forming a multitude of gateways, each lasting only a second, while
the light brown trunks of the immense trees soared up into
the green night sky—in fact, their fused crowns *were* the sky.
Mitya flew between the blades of grass, constantly changing
course, and ahead of him appeared ever new corridors of
swaying triumphal arches. The grass glowed in the dark when
it was bent over by the wind, or perhaps the glow appeared
in the air every time one of the stems moved through it, as
though the shifting grass were scratching light out of darkness.

Down below, life continued its monotonous motions, with
myriads of different-colored insects crawling over the ground,
each pushing a sphere of dung. Some of them opened their
wings and attempted to fly, but only a few managed it, and
even they fell back almost immediately to earth under the
weight of their spheres. Most of the insects were moving in
the same direction, toward a clearing flooded with light,
which could sometimes be glimpsed through the gaps between the blades of grass. Mitya flew in that direction, too,
and soon he saw ahead of him a large tree stump from some

southern tree which he didn't recognize. Completely rotten, it glowed in the darkness. The entire clearing in front of it was covered with a colorful shifting carpet of insects. They were gazing spellbound at the stump, which emitted waves of charismatic energy that transformed it into the sole and incontrovertible source of meaning and light in the universe. Somehow or other Mitya understood that these waves were nothing more than a reflection of the attention of all the insects who had gathered there in the clearing to see the tree stump.

Flying a little closer, he could make out a small group of insects standing on the perimeter of the stump facing the clearing. It was a varied group, including beautiful timber beetles with mosaics on their chitin wing cases, black praying mantises with their front feet clasped in supplication, wasps, gleaming scarabs, numerous dragonflies, and butterflies with colorful wings. Behind them he could see several dull-gray spiders who didn't expose themselves too much to the view of the insects gathered below. He couldn't see what was happening in the very center of the stump, and this induced a sense of dark mystery, as though some terrible and mighty insect was sitting there—an insect so all-powerful that none was permitted to see him, leaving them only to hope that he was benevolent. The insects on the edge of the stump were waving their front legs gently to and fro, as though conducting some soundless music, and the huge crowd gathered below was swaying in time to their movements, which seemed to follow an inaudible musical phrase with such precision that Mitya could almost hear it, as though a distant organ were pealing a melody which would have been truly sublime if it weren't interrupted every now and then by an absurd "oompah-oompah." But Mitya only had to look away from the stump and the crowd of insects rhythmically swaying around it to know immediately that he was surrounded by silence.

Mitya rose high into the air until the stump was directly below him, and he could see what was happening in its center. He almost went out of his mind at the sight, especially when he remembered the many exposés of the stump's varied mysteries in the newspapers sold by the ants in the deep, dark pedestrian passageways of the metro system that they themselves had dug. Mitya looked down and shuddered.

In the center of the stump was a puddle, with several rotten twigs floating in it. More precisely, this wasn't even the center itself: the stump was so rotten there was nothing left of it but bark, and immediately behind it was a pit of decay, filled with foul water.

Mitya imagined what would happen when the bark cracked and the water flooded over the living carpet swaying in front of the stump, and he was horrified. Then he noticed that the light emitted by the stump flickered in a strange fashion, as though someone were turning it on and off at incredible speed, each time catching a crowd of plaster-cast insects in the darkness, almost the same as those which had been there a moment before, but just a little different.

Down below, an uninterrupted stream of insects hurried toward the stump, pressing in on those who had already traveled this route and trampling them into the ground, as though the multicolored living carpet was stretching toward the stump and folding back under itself. Insects jumped up on the stump, and most of them lost their grip and tumbled back down, under the legs, pincers, and antennae of others who were crawling in from all sides to take their place, but some managed to climb up and join the insects standing on the green glowing rim. They scrambled up as quickly as they could and immediately turned around like the others, avoiding at all costs looking at what was at the center of the stump; then they began conducting, keeping up a continuous melody.

Mitya flew away. There was no one for him to tell that this stump and all the insects who had gathered on it were by no means everything in the world, and this made him feel sad, and he felt even sadder because he himself was not entirely sure. But when he reached the edge of the clearing he saw the diffused light emitted by the grass, and he remembered how he'd felt before he reached the clearing with the rotten stump, and calmed down. Once again, the triumphal arches of the bowed stems of grass rushed past above his head, and the farther he flew from the clearing, the fewer insects he saw below him. Soon there were none at all, and then flowers began to appear. They seemed to be especially planted beds of unusual varieties, but they gave out such a stupefying scent that Mitya preferred to admire them from a distance, especially as there were bees who had retired from the world crawling about on some of them, and he did not wish to intrude on their isolation.

Mitya glimpsed a red light ahead of him through the grass, and automatically turned toward it. When he was close enough for everything around him to be surrounded by a reddish reflected glow, he flew stealthily, hovering for long periods behind broad blades of grass, flitting imperceptibly from one to another. After repeating this maneuver several times, he glanced out from behind a stem and very close, almost under his very nose, he saw two very strange red beetles, unlike any he had seen before. They had large yellow growths like wide-brimmed straw hats on their heads, and as far as Mitya could tell, the undersides of their abdomens were khaki-colored. They were sitting absolutely motionless on a blade of grass, gazing thoughtfully into the distance and swaying only slightly with the motion of the plant itself.

"I think," said one of the beetles, "that there is nothing in the world higher than our solitude."

"If we don't count the eucalyptuses," said the other.

"And the plane trees," the first beetle added, after a moment's thought.

"And the chicle tree," said his companion.

"The chicle tree?"

"Yes, the chicle tree, which grows in the southeastern part of Yucatán."

"I suppose so," agreed the first beetle. "But that rotten old stump in the clearing is certainly not higher than our solitude."

"That is certain," said the second beetle.

Once again, they gazed thoughtfully into the distance.

"What new dreams have you seen?" the first beetle asked after a few minutes of silence.

"Many," said the second beetle. "Today, for instance, I discovered a distant and very strange world, where someone had also seen us."

"Could that be?" asked the first beetle.

"Yes," replied the second. "But he who saw us took us for two red lamps on a mountain peak by the sea."

"And what did we do in your dream?" asked the first beetle.

The second paused dramatically. "We shone," he said with Indian solemnity, "until the electricity was turned off."

"Yes," said the first beetle. "Our spirit is indeed beyond reproach."

"Most certainly," said the second. "But most interesting of all is the fact that he who caught sight of us has flown directly here and is hiding behind the next blade of grass."

"Can this be true?" inquired the first beetle.

"Of course," said the second. "But you know it yourself."

"And what does he intend to do?" asked the first beetle.

"He intends," said the second, "to jump into well number one."

"This is interesting," said the first beetle, "but why well number one? He might equally choose well number three."

"Yes," replied the second, "or well number nine."

"Or even well number fourteen," said the first beetle.

"But it is best of all," said the second, "to jump into well number forty-eight."

Mitya pressed himself tight against the stem, listening as the numbers increased just a few feet away from him, and then a hand was placed on his shoulder and he was shaken powerfully.

Turning his head, he saw Dima leaning over him. They were on the ledge at the top of the mountain, with the mast with the two red lamps, no longer lit, rising above them. Two folding stools lay beside them, and Mitya was lying under a bush.

"Get up," said Dima. "We don't have much time."

Mitya stood up and shook his head in an attempt to remember the dream he had just had, but it had already evaporated, leaving behind nothing but a vague and indefinite sensation.

Dima set off along a narrow path leading away from the mast with the two red lamps. Mitya plodded after him, still yawning, but after they had walked a few feet and the path had become a narrow ledge with nothing below it but a drop down to the sea, the tattered remnants of sleep abandoned him totally. The path dipped into a crevice between the rocks, passed under a low stone arch (here Mitya vaguely recalled something to do with his dream), and led them out into a narrow ravine overgrown with dark bushes. Mitya picked a few cold sloes, tossed them into his mouth, and spat them out when he saw a white skull lying under the bush. The skull was small and narrow, like a dog's.

"There!" said Dima, pointing at the bushes.

"What?" asked Mitya.

"The well."

"What well?" asked Mitya.

"The well you must look into."

"What for?"

"It's the only entrance and exit," said Dima.

"Where to?"

"In order to answer that," said Dima, "you have to look into the well. Then you'll see everything for yourself."

"What is all this?"

"I think you know what a well is," said Dima.

"Yes, I do. A contrivance for drawing water out of the earth."

"And what else? You spoke to me once about cities and a well. You said something about cities being replaced, but the wells always remaining the same."

"I remember. It's the forty-eighth hexagram," said Mitya, and again he had the idea there had been something similar in his dream. "That's what it's called, 'The Well.' 'Cities they change, but they do not change the well. You will lose nothing, but neither will you gain anything. You will depart and return, but the well remains a well . . . If you almost reach the water, but the rope is too short, or if you break the bucket—misfortune!' "

"Where's that from," asked Dima.

"The *I Ching*, or *Book of Changes*."

"Do you know it by heart, then?"

"No," Mitya confessed in a dissatisfied voice. "It's just that I was given that hexagram five times."

"How interesting. And what's it about?"

"About a well. About the existence of a certain well that can be used. Or rather, at first it can't be used, because at the first position there is no water in it, at the second the water cannot be drawn, and at the third there is no one to drink it. But then everything works out, unless I've got things confused. The meaning is roughly that we carry within ourselves the source of everything that can possibly exist, but the source is not accessible from the first, second, and third positions because they symbolize inadequate levels of development. And it is also symbolic that we arrive at this hexagram from the hexagram 'Exhaustion,' at the fifth position of which . . ."

"That's enough," Dima interrupted. "Remember the song that we heard on the boardwalk? About where to find yourself? The woman singing it didn't understand a single thing she was singing. And you don't understand a thing you're talking about. In order to understand what you've just said, you have to look into the well."

"What if I don't go?"

"You simply can't not go."

"Why?" asked Mitya.

Dima looked at Mitya's hands. Mitya followed his glance and realized that his hands no longer glowed in the dark. A few minutes ago, when they set out for this place, his hands were still glowing, not as brightly as the day before, but still with a pure and clear blue light.

"That's why," said Dima. "Otherwise, everything you have understood will just disappear. And the best you can hope for is to write another couple of verse missives to mosquitoes who have absolutely no need for them."

"Sometimes I find your self-assurance quite staggering," said Mitya.

Dima turned him around and pushed him in the back.

The bushes were dense and prickly. Mitya put his hands over his eyes and took a few steps. Then he began tumbling down through the air.

He fell with his back facing down, clutching at the crumbling walls, fell for a very long time—but instead of falling to the bottom, he fell into a state of profound thought.

Time did not so much disappear as stretch out. Everything that he saw changed without changing, somehow constantly becoming new, and his fingers kept on clutching at the same section of wall as at the beginning of his fall. Like the day before, he felt as though he was looking at something strange, something he had never looked at in his life, and yet something he had always been looking at. When he attempted to understand what it was he saw, and discover something similar in his memory, he recalled a snippet of a film he had seen once on television, in which several scientists in white coats were involved in very strange work. They were cutting circles with small projections out of cardboard and threading them on a gleaming metal rod, as though they were receipts in a shop. The cardboard circles gradually grew smaller and smaller, until finally the form on the metal rod was a human head composed of thin layers of cardboard. They smeared it with blue plaster, and that was the end of the film.

What Mitya saw now reminded him most of all of those

cardboard circles. The very last of the circles was his fright when he fell into the well, and the one before that was his fear that a prickly branch would lash into his eyes, and before that there was his annoyance that the world of his dream, where the two red beetles conversed on a long blade of grass, had disappeared so quickly. Even earlier there was his fear of the bat, the delight in flying over the rocks flooded with moonlight, the struggle with Dima's incomprehensible question, the depression induced by the tapping of the dominoes on the deserted boardwalk, and even more by the immediate appearance of a chattering group of domino players in his own head—and so on, lower and lower, on through his entire life, through all the compressed and fossilized feelings he had ever experienced.

At first Mitya decided that he was seeing himself, but he immediately realized that nothing the well contained had any connection with him at all. He was not this well, he was the person who fell into it, at the same time staying exactly where he was. Perhaps he was the plaster binding together the super-thin layers of feelings which were overlaid one on top of the other. He passed through all the meaningless snapshots of his life leading back to the point of birth, and when he reached it and tried to go further to find the beginning, he realized he was staring into eternity.

There was no bottom to the well. There never was a beginning.

Then Mitya noticed another thing: nothing in the well below the point from which he was accustomed to begin his personal accounting was in the least bit frightening, not the world beyond the grave or the world on this side of the grave—a nice phrase, he thought—nor the least bit mysterious or strange. It had always been there beside him, closer than beside him, and he hadn't remembered it because it was just that which did the remembering.

"Hey!" he heard a distant voice call. "Come on out! That's enough. Don't go breaking the bucket."

He felt himself being pulled by the arm, then a branch with sharp thorns brushed across his face, black leaves flashed in front of his eyes, and he saw Dima standing in front of him.

"Let's get out of here," said Dima.

"What was that?" asked Mitya.

"A well," said Dima, as though revealing some great secret.

"Will I ever fall into it again?"

Dima stopped and looked at him in astonishment. "We can't fall into a well where we've already spent an eternity. We can only climb out of it."

"And have I climbed out of it now?"

"Not now, but then. You're back in it again now. You stuck your head out. Life is structured very strangely. In order to get out of the well, you have to fall into it."

"But what for?"

"You can bring something back from the well. It contains priceless treasures. Or rather, it doesn't actually contain anything, you come out just the same as when you went in. But while you're in there you may notice what you have and what you forgot about a long time ago."

Mitya withdrew into deep reflection and walked the rest of the way in silence.

"I didn't notice any treasures in there," he said when they were back at the ledge under the beacon. "I simply saw my entire life in the space of a second. And more."

"A lifetime and more, as you put it, only exists for a fleeting moment. The one which is happening right now. This is the priceless treasure which you found. And now you can fit everything you wish into one fleeting moment: your own life, and anyone else's."

"But I can't see what I've found," said Mitya.

"Because you've found what sees," Dima replied. "Close your eyes and look."

"Where?"

"Wherever you like."

Mitya closed his eyes and in the darkness which descended he saw a bright blue point of light. It was motionless, but in some strange way he could direct it onto anything he chose.

Mitya heard the rasping song of a cicada, directed his blue point of light toward the insect, and suddenly he was remembering an evening long before, when he first stood on his own feet. It happened very early, immediately after he hatched from the egg and fell to the earth from the branch of the tree in which he began his existence.

PARADISE

Seryozha couldn't remember his parents. He had stood on his own feet from a very early age, immediately after he had hatched from the egg and fallen to the ground from a branch of the tree in which he had begun his existence. It happened against the backdrop of an incredibly beautiful sunset on a windless summer evening, with the sea murmuring and the cicadas singing in chorus. One day he could become a cicada, too, but the prospect seemed so vague and so far away that he didn't even consider it; he realized that if it was his fate to trill his song on sounding lamellae, then it would not be him doing it, or not quite him, because these lamellae grow only on certain individuals, on those who have spent many years journeying under the ground and have finally managed to break out to the surface, clamber onto a tree, and hatch completely. For some reason, he was quite sure that if it happened to him it would also be on a summer evening, one just as calm and warm as this one.

Seryozha bit his way into the earth, trying then and there to get used to the idea that this was a serious, long-term business. He knew the chances of making it back to the surface were very small and the only things he could rely on to help him were sobriety and presence of mind and the ability to keep digging longer than the others, and the thought that the others understood that, too, gave him extra strength. But childhood is childhood, and he spent his first few years aimlessly examining the objects he came across in the soil. Some of them he could take out and turn over in his hands, but some he had to examine where they lay. Seryozha especially loved finding windows: he would thrust his fingers into the earth and carefully feel the cold hard surface, then clean it off, trying to guess what he would see behind the glass.

The experience of all those years spent creeping through the soft Russian loam (which one morning suddenly turned out to be the noble black earth of Ukraine) fused into one single promising memory, of himself shuddering with the frosty cold as he looked in at a newly cleaned window and saw the black gloom of winter gathered around a brightly lit children's playground, and in a circle of light in the center there was a snow woman with a coronet of carrots stuck on her head, looking like the Statue of Liberty he'd seen in a magazine he had dug up not far from the window. The glass was covered in a tracery of frost, with a pattern very much like a small grove of palm trees. The palms seemed to sway as he breathed on them. It was impossible to climb through the window, and Seryozha stood beside it for a long time, yearning for something he couldn't explain, and then he began digging his tunnel again, carrying the undeciphered dream in his heart.

By the time he began wondering whether he was doing everything right, his life had become a routine consisting for the most part of events very much like each other repeated in a monotonous sequence. Ahead of him, directly in front of his face and shoulders, there was a circle of dark firm earth. Behind him was the tunnel he had dug so far, but Seryozha never looked back and never counted how many feet he had come. He knew that other insects, ants for instance, were happy with a fairly short burrow and could carry out their life's work in a few hours using the serrated edges of their legs. But he never dwelt on such comparisons, aware that once he stopped and began to compare himself with others, it would begin to seem that he had already achieved a great deal, and he would lose the sense of resentment toward life that was essential to continue his struggle.

His achievements did not exist in a form which could be touched or added up; they consisted of the meetings and events which each new day brought. When he woke in the morning, he went on digging his tunnel, raking out the earth with his powerful front legs and using his back legs to push it aside. After a few minutes, breakfast would appear among the gray-brown clumps of earth, in the form of thin shoots or roots, from which Seryozha sucked out the juice while he read some newspaper or other that he usually unearthed together with his food. A few inches farther on, the door to work would appear out of the earth—in fact, the distance from breakfast to the door was so short that sometimes the earth crumbled away on its own without his needing to make any effort. Seryozha could not figure out how he could keep digging in the same direction and still unearth the door to work every morning, but he understood that pondering such matters never did any good, and so he preferred not to think about it.

Behind the doors to work Seryozha found his listless, earth-encrusted colleagues, and he had to move past them very slowly, so that they wouldn't realize he was digging a tunnel. Perhaps they were all digging their own tunnels, too, but if so, they did it very secretively. Seryozha scraped the earth off his drawing board, cleaned the window which offered a view of pipes extending up, and began unhurriedly digging his way toward lunch. Lunch was virtually the same as breakfast, only the dirt surrounding it was a little different, more crumbly, with the slow-chewing faces of his colleagues protruding from it, but this didn't upset him, because their eyes were always closed. Lunch was more or less the high point of the day, and afterward he began digging the tunnel back home, and the digging in that direction always went quickly. After a while, Seryozha unearthed the door to his flat, slowly scraped away the clay behind which he discovered the television, and a couple of hours later, half asleep, he dug his way to bed.

When he woke up, he usually turned toward the wall and looked at it for a while, trying to remember the dream that had just ended, and then with a few swift blows of his hands he broke a passage through into the bathroom. By and large, the days were all identical, except that on Saturday and Sunday Seryozha's constant forward progress did not bring him up against the door into work. Sometimes on weekends he unearthed a bottle or two of vodka, and then he would dig a bit more in the dirt around him. Almost always he exposed the head and part of the body of one of his friends, and they would have a drink together and talk about life. Seryozha knew quite definitely that most of his acquaintances were not digging a tunnel, but even so, they turned up with oppressive monotony.

Sometimes, it was true, there were pleasant surprises in the earth: for instance, there might be the lower half of a female torso protruding from the wall (Seryozha never unearthed women above the waist, believing that this would only cause problems), or a couple of cans of beer, in honor of which he would allow himself a little break, but most of his path was traveled in working. In order to have some kind of explanation for the strange fact that although he always moved in the same direction by the compass he often dug his way through beds of earth with identical items embedded in them, like the drawing desks, his colleagues, and even the view from a window, Seryozha made an analogy with a train moving forward, constantly approaching the ultimate sleeper, which was indistinguishable from the others beside it.

But there were certain differences: sometimes the office through which Seryozha made his daily dig would change, the drawing desks were rearranged, the color of the walls was different, someone appeared for the first time or disappeared forever.

His work was not difficult at all, he had to redraw old blueprints: several other employees did the same thing. In the morning they usually struck up a long unhurried conversation, and it was impossible not to join in. They spoke in the usual manner about everything under the sun, but since the range of topics they dealt with was very limited, Seryozha noticed that with every day that passed there was less under the sun than there had been before—less than there had been, for instance, that evening when he sat under the branch and listened to the song of the cicadas who had dug their way out from underground.

This unavoidable social intercourse with his colleagues had a bad effect on Seryozha. He began crawling differently, pressing his head hard against the earth, and sometimes when he was unearthing the long staircase down to the buffet, he used his face as well as his hands. He also began to regard life in a different light. His previous desire to dig his tunnel as far as possible began to give way to a sense of responsibility for his future, and this feeling produced purely anatomical changes.

Once he noticed that he was sitting at his desk, using both hands to sharpen a pencil and at the same time rummaging in the drawer with something that he simply didn't have before. At first he was sure he was going insane, but when he looked more closely at his colleagues he began noticing that they, too, had barely visible, semitransparent brown limbs along their sides which they used very skillfully. Once he had learned to see these limbs, he, too, began learning to use them. At first they were weak, but gradually they grew stronger, and Seryozha began to trust them to do his work while he used his hands for their real function of digging the tunnel farther and farther.

But, even so, every day the tunnel brought him to work,

where the same old faces in which every feature was familiar gazed out from the crumbly earth of the walls. They all had one feature in common: all of them had mustaches. Seryozha never thought this particularly significant, but he decided to try growing one for himself anyway.

About a month later, when his whiskers had grown quite long, he noticed that life was now somehow fuller, while his colleagues had turned into remarkably nice guys with the most varied interests. It was the mustaches which helped him to understand this, because their groping movements gave him an understanding of life from a side he had never been aware of before. He became convinced that, with the help of a mustache, life could not only be seen but also felt, so that it becomes so fascinating that there's no particular point in digging a tunnel any farther. He began to take an interest in his surroundings, but even more interesting was what others thought of him.

Then one day after work, as he drank cognac at a party, he heard someone say: "At last, Sergei, you've become one of us."

The words were spoken by one particular face barely protruding from the wall of earth. The other faces closed their eyes and began groping with their mustaches, as if they were feeling Seryozha to check that he really was one of them. To judge from their smiles, they were satisfied with the answer.

"But what have I become?" asked Seryozha.

"Stop pretending," chuckled the faces. "As if you didn't know."

"No, really," Seryozha persisted. "What?"

"Why, a cockroach, who else?"

Seryozha felt a cold shudder run right through him. He dashed to the end of the tunnel and began feverishly thrusting aside the earth, to the sound of hoots and laughter from the bewhiskered faces behind him. When he unearthed the door of the bathroom, he rapidly dug a passage to the mirror, looked at the brown triangular face with the long swaying whiskers, and grabbed his razor. The mustache came away with a crunch, and Seryozha saw his own face looking out at him, only now it was a completely adult face with obvious wrinkles around the eyes. "How long was I a cockroach?" he thought in horror, remembering the oath he had taken in his childhood to dig a passage to the surface.

He unearthed his bed, dropped onto its cold sheets, and fell asleep, and in the morning he unearthed the telephone and called Grisha, one of his friends from the ovipositor days whom he hadn't seen for ages. They spent a while reminiscing about that distant summer evening when they fell from the branch to the earth and began to dig a passage to its surface, and then Seryozha bluntly asked how he should live his life from now on. His friend told him: "Dig up as much cash as you can, and then you'll see for yourself."

They arranged to meet sometime and said goodbye. After he hung up, Seryozha unhesitatingly decided to change his route and follow Grisha's advice. After breakfast he began digging to the right instead of straight ahead, and was relieved to notice that no doors to work appeared in the earth in front of him. Instead, he came across an old German army helmet with holes in it and a photocopy of some ancient mystical book, which he spent a couple of hours poring over. Seryozha had never read this kind of nonsense before: the book suggested that not only was he crawling through an underground tunnel, he was also pushing a sphere of dung along in front of him, and he was really digging his tunnel inside the sphere of dung. After that, the earth was completely empty for a long distance, with nothing but fine roots here and there, which Seryozha used for food, until eventually his hand encountered something solid as he thrust it into the earth.

Tossing aside the yellow clay, Seryozha saw the black stocking of a military man's boot. He knew immediately what to do. He carefully sprinkled dirt back over the boot and began digging to the left, to get as far away from the spot as possible. On other occasions he encountered items of military equipment projecting from the earth—clubs, walkie-talkies, shaved heads in peaked caps. He was lucky with the heads, because he always unearthed them from the back, so the pigs couldn't see him. After a while he began coming across cash in the dirt. At first it was just isolated notes, but then whole bundles began to appear, usually not too far away from a beat cop's club or boot. Seryozha began working painstakingly, like an archaeologist, clearing away the earth from the pieces of military equipment he encountered, and it was a rare occasion when he crawled away without several heavy, wet bundles of bills wrapped in strips of paper.

He began to be less careful, and once an accidental movement of his hand swept away the dirt from the round face of a military man with a whistle stuck in its lips. The face glared at him and inflated its cheeks, but before a sound emerged, Seryozha tugged the whistle out of its mouth and stuck a packet of cash in its place. The face closed its eyes and Seryozha moved on, gradually recovering his composure. Soon his fingers encountered another object which felt like a militiaman's boot. Clearing away the earth, Seryozha saw the word Reebok. He dug upward and soon unearthed Grisha's face.

"Nice to see you at last," said Grisha.

The cash Seryozha had dug up on his advice made not the slightest impression on Grisha.

"Use it to buy money before it's too late," Grisha advised him, and he showed Seryozha several green bills.

"And anyway, you've got to dig out of here as quickly as you can."

Seryozha himself realized that there was nowhere he could dig out of apart from here; however, he took Grisha's words to heart and remembered that first he had to dig up an invitation.

On his route through the earth he still regularly encountered the front door, the television, the bathroom, and the kitchen, but now he began digging up American magazines and studying English, which he spoke with faces that appeared out of the walls very occasionally. The faces smiled in a friendly fashion and promised to help him. Then one day, in a long vein of sand that he had been working through for a month, he came across a white piece of paper folded into squares and realized that this was the invitation. Seryozha didn't know what to do next, and he decided to stick to the vein of sand and see what happened. He didn't come across anything interesting for several days and then he reached a stone wall with a sign that read: FOREIGN VISA DEPARTMENT. After that, he began finding things at an astounding speed—he didn't even really have time to take in what it was he unearthed and who it was he bribed. Eventually Seryozha noticed that, rather than a fat bag of cash, he now had several green pieces of paper with a picture of some good-looking, overweight individual on them.

The vein of sand came to an end, and digging the passage became much more difficult, because the soil was stony now. Seryozha never forgot the blocks of concrete just before the American embassy. They were so big that he either had to dig his way under them (which was dangerous, because they could fall and crush him) or he had to dig around them to the side, which made his route much longer. Seryozha crawled through the embassy quickly, however, unearthed the handrail of the steps leading into an airplane, cleaned the earth from the small round window, and spent almost an entire day admiring the clouds and the ocean.

After that came a layer of crumbly, damp red loam. Seryozha gazed for a long time at this wall which concealed the unknown before he reached out his calloused and weary but still strong hands. His first discovery in the new soil was an elderly black woman in a customs service booth, who fastidiously inquired whether Seryozha had a return ticket. Then came the door of a bus, behind which Seryozha immediately unearthed an apple core and a crumpled map of New York.

A new life began. For a long time Seryozha unearthed

mostly empty tin cans, stale pizza crusts, and old copies of *Reader's Digest*, but he had prepared himself for hard work and was not expecting any manna from the heavens, especially since the heavens were in short supply underground. After some time, he began to find money as well. Of course, there was a lot less of it than the amounts of Russian cash he used to find, and it didn't turn up in bundles, but Seryozha didn't lose heart. Often there were huge plastic bags of rubbish sticking out of the walls, or hands holding out small bags of cocaine or invitations to talks on religion, but Seryozha tried to take no notice, to smile as much as possible and generally be optimistic.

Gradually the amount of rubbish decreased, and one quiet morning, as Seryozha was struggling to dig his way between the roots of an old lime tree, he discovered a small green card. This was just one day after he learned his second important American word, "oops" (the first one, "bla-bla-bla," had been told to him in secret by Grisha much earlier). He realized that now he would be able to find work, and only a couple of days later, shortly after breakfast, Seryozha unearthed a metal door with an illuminated sign reading: *Work*. He swallowed hard to control his excitement and got going. The new work proved to be very like his old job, only the drawing desk was different, with a rolled top, and the faces of his colleagues sticking out of the wall all spoke English. When he dug his way from lunch to the sign which read: *Don't Work* (he had long ago managed to combine time and space into a single whole), he realized that the working day was over.

Now Seryozha unearthed the signs *Work* and *Don't Work* every day; he also began to have regular encounters with the same gleaming doorknobs, steps, and household items such as an air conditioner, which filled everywhere with its buzzing and reminded him slightly of a snowstorm in Moscow. All of which prompted the conclusion that he was now living in his own apartment.

His work was not at all difficult. He had to translate old blueprints into computer code, which was what several other employees also did. In the morning they usually struck up a long unhurried conversation in English, in which Seryozha gradually learned to participate. This association with his colleagues undoubtedly had a very good effect on him. He began to crawl in a more confident manner, and soon he noticed that he was again using the semitransparent legs that he had forgotten about since he left his last job. He grew whiskers again (this time with a clear touch of gray), not in order to blend in with his fellows, although most of them did have whiskers, but in order to lend his own face that inimitable quality of individuality which each of them possessed.

Several years went by, filled with the alternate flickering of the signs *Work / Don't Work*. During this time Seryozha put down roots and dug up a whole series of useful objects, including a car, a huge television, and even a toilet with a long-distance flush mechanism. Sometimes when he was at work in the daytime, he would unearth the window of his office, open it, and paying no attention to the stifling heat that came rushing in, he would stick out his hand with the long-distance flush mechanism and press the black button marked with a waterfall. Nothing seemed to happen, but he knew that in his apartment two miles away a roaring whirlpool of bluish water was swirling down the cool sides of the toilet bowl. Once Seryozha pressed the "reset" button by mistake, and then spent three days washing off the floor, ceiling, and walls, but then after a fierce argument with a short scarab who called himself the landlord, he began to treat the apartment as though it was alive. In any case, its name, Van Bedroom, had always sounded to him like a Dutch artist.

Sometimes Seryozha unearthed a leash, from which he drew the conclusion that he was walking a dog. He never did unearth the dog itself, but he once followed the advice of *Health Week* magazine and took it to a veterinary psychoanalyst, who spent some time exchanging barks with the invisible animal behind a thin wall of earth, and then told Seryozha things which made him tie the leash to the protruding bumper of an out-of-state truck, look around—of course there was no one else there—and dig hurriedly away from the spot.

On weekends he dug as far as the ferry to New Jersey, unearthed the little window where they sold tickets, and recalled his childhood as he looked at the distant Statue of Liberty. The dying rays of the setting sun tinted the crown on her head red, and she looked like a huge middle-aged snow maiden decorated with gigantic carrots.

Seryozha acquired a woman friend, whom he unearthed completely for rare conversations on subjects close to his heart—by this stage, he had quite a lot of them.

"Do you believe," he would ask, "that there is light for us at the end of the tunnel?"

"Are you asking me what comes after death?" she asked. "I don't know. I read a couple of books about it. They write about a tunnel with a light at the end of it, but I think it's all just a load of bla-bla-bla."

When he told her that he had almost become a cockroach in a distant northern country, he roused a smile of disbelief, and she said he didn't look anything like a Russian exile.

"You look just like a typical American cockroach," she said.

"Oo-oops," said Seryozha.

He was happy that he'd become so naturalized in his new home, and he accepted the English word "cockroach" as something like the term "cockney," New York style, but even so, her words left him with an uneasy feeling. One day after work, when he'd drunk quite a lot, Seryozha unearthed his apartment, dug a passage to the mirror, glanced into it, and shuddered at what he saw. Staring back at him was the triangular brown head with long whiskers that he had seen a long time ago. Seryozha grabbed his razor, and when the soapy whirlpool in the washbasin had carried away the last of the whiskers, he saw his own face looking out at him, but now it was distinctly elderly, almost old. He began digging frenziedly straight through the mirror, which shattered into fragments beneath his hands, and soon he unearthed a number of items which indicated that he was in fact out on the street—they included an old Korean sitting on a stool, and a sign which read: "East 29th Street." Cutting himself on a rusty tin can, he began digging quickly and desperately straight ahead, until he found himself in a vein of damp clayey soil somewhere around Greenwich Village, surrounded by foundations that sank deep into the earth and concrete shafts. He unearthed a signboard with a picture of a palm grove and the word PARADISE in big letters. Behind it Seryozha discovered a longish staircase leading downward, a stool, a short length of a bar, and two glasses of the vodka tonic he had grown accustomed to.

The earthen walls of the tunnel he had just dug were throbbing with the sound of music. Seryozha downed the two glasses one after the other and took a look around. Behind him there was a long narrow passage filled with loosened earth. It led back into the familiar world from which Seryozha had been trying to find a way out all these years. In front of him, the scratched wooden top of the bar protruded from the earth, with glasses standing on it. He still couldn't tell whether he'd managed to find a way out or not. And out of what, in any case? That was the most difficult thing to understand. Seryozha picked a pale green matchbox bearing the word PARADISE from the counter, and saw the same palms that were on the sign, the same palms he'd seen drawn in frost on a window in his childhood. As well as the palms, the matchbox had telephone numbers, an address, and an assurance that this was "the hottest place on the island."

"My God," thought Seryozha, "is heaven the hottest place? And not the other place?"

A hand appeared out of the wall of earth in front of him, scooped up the empty glasses, and set down a full one. Trying to keep his self-control, Seryozha looked up. As usual, the vault of earth hung only a foot above his head, and Seryozha suddenly realized that in all the long and full life he'd spent digging, he'd probably never even once tried digging up. He thrust his hands into the ceiling, and the earth quickly began piling up on the floor. He pulled over a stool, stood on it, and a minute later his fingers encountered empty space. "Of course," thought Seryozha, "the surface is the place where you don't have to dig anymore! And where there's no more earth, there's no need to dig!" He heard fingers snapping down below, and tossed down his wallet with its small deck of credit cards—at the point where he had been sitting, there was now a huge, motionless dark gray sphere that had appeared out of nowhere. Then he grabbed hold of the edge of the hole and pulled himself up and out.

It was a windless summer evening, with the purple clouds of sunset gleaming through the leaves of the trees. The sea was murmuring gently in the distance, and the sound of cicadas singing surrounded him on all sides. Ripping open his old skin, Seryozha climbed out of it and looked up. On the tree growing over his head, he saw the branch from which he had fallen to earth. Seryozha realized it was the same evening that he had begun his long underground journey, because there simply is no other evening, and he also understood what the cicadas were singing, or rather crying, about. He set his broad lamellae singing of the fact that life had passed in vain, and that it could only pass in vain, and there was no point in weeping over it. Then he straightened his wings and flew off toward the purple glow above the distant mountain, trying to rid himself of the feeling that he was digging through the air with his wings. He was still clutching something, and when he raised it to his eyes he saw on his palm the crumpled and earth-stained little box with the black palm trees, and suddenly he realized that the word PARADISE means the place people go when they die.

THREE FEELINGS OF

A YOUNG MOTHER

As she finished her last bruised plum, Marina felt absolutely no concern for the future. She was certain that at night she would find everything she needed at the market. But when she decided to go out and see whether it was night outside, and crawled down off the pile of straw that her weight had flattened, she saw that there was no way out to the market, and remembered that Nikolai had blocked it off almost immediately after he had appeared. He had done such a good job that not a trace was left, and Marina could not even remember where the way out used to be. She looked around in desperation. An icy wind blew in through the black hole in front of which Nikolai's woven mat lay on the floor, but the other three walls were absolutely identical, black and damp. Marina didn't have the strength to begin digging the passage all over again and she fell back on the straw, sobbing helplessly. In the French film there had been no suggestion that such a turn of events was even possible, and Marina had no idea what to do.

After a good cry, she calmed down a little. She wasn't particularly hungry and she still had the two heavy bundles she had brought back from the theater. She decided to bring them through to the chamber, and squeezed into the black hole and along the narrow crooked passage, in which the snow had built up. After the first few feet she realized that it was very difficult for her to crawl; her sides kept catching on the walls. Feeling herself with her hands, she realized with horror that in the few days she had spent lying on the straw recovering from the shock of Nikolai's death, she had grown incredibly fat. Her waist and the place where her wings used to be had expanded most, and now they were genuine bags of fat. In one particular narrow section of the corridor, Marina got stuck and thought she would never get out, but after a long struggle she managed to crawl all the way to the exit. The accordion and the bundles were where she had left them, but they were covered with snow; Marina decided not to bring the accordion back, and she took only the bundles, using the accordion to brace the covering of the entrance from the inside.

After scrambling back somehow or other to her place, Marina looked wearily at the gray newspapers covering the bundles. She could guess what she would find inside, and was in no hurry to open them. The paper bore the title *Magadan Ant* in large, pseudo-Slavonic script, and above that the motto "Long live our Magadan anthill," in Gothic italics. Lower down there was a photograph, but Marina couldn't tell what exactly it showed because of the crust of dried blood that covered the lower half of the bundle. The only thing she could make out from the subheads was that this was a Sunday issue which was mostly devoted to cultural matters. Marina was tormented by an unfamiliar physical sensation, and she decided to read for a while to settle down. She cautiously turned back the top of the page and saw the columns of text on the other side.

The first article, entitled "Motherhood," was written by a Major Bugaev. When her eyes lit on the word, Marina felt her heart skip a beat. She began reading with as much concentration as she was capable of.

"When we come into this life," wrote the major, "we do not wonder where we have come from and what we were before. We do not ponder why it has happened, we simply crawl along the boardwalk, gazing around and listening to the waves gently lapping at the shore."

Marina sighed and thought how well the major knew life.

"But the day arrives," she read, "and we learn how the world is arranged, and we understand that our first responsibility to the natural world and to society is to give life to new generations of ants who will continue our great cause and write new and glorious pages in our centuries-old history. This is the context in which I feel I must deal with the feelings of the young mother. First, she feels a deep tenderness for the eggs she has laid, which is expressed in constant care and attention. Second, she feels a vague sadness as the result of constant reflection on the fate of her offspring, which is so often unpredictable in the modern world. Third, she feels a joyful pride in the awareness . . ."

The final word ran into the dry brown crust, and Marina looked across to the next column, screwing up her eyes to control a torrent of unfamiliar feelings.

"For the Latvian Communist Party I was something of a Cassandra," she began reading, then dropped the newspaper.

"I'm pregnant," she said aloud.

•

Marina laid her first egg without even realizing it, in her sleep. She was dreaming that she was a young ant female once again, building a shelter of snow in the yard of the Magadan Opera House. First she made a small snowball and then rolled it around in the snow, so that it gradually became bigger and bigger, but for some reason it wasn't round but very long, and no matter how Marina tried, she couldn't make it any rounder.

When she woke, she saw she had thrown off the blanket as she tossed around in her sleep, and now she was lying on the straw, and where Nikolai's boots used to stand there was a white object which was exactly the same shape as the strange snowball in her dream. Marina moved, and another egg tumbled down to the floor. She leaped up in fright, and her body began shuddering in uncontrollable but virtually painless spasms. A few more eggs fell to the floor. They were identical, white and cold, covered with a dull elastic skin and shaped like medium-sized melons. There were seven of them altogether.

"Now what do I do?" Marina thought anxiously, and suddenly she knew: the first thing to be done was to hollow out a niche for the eggs.

Throwing aside the soil with the trowel, Marina paid close attention to what she was feeling, and was astonished that she did not feel the joy in motherhood described by Major Bugaev. Her only feelings were concern that the recess might be too cold, and a slight revulsion for the newly laid eggs.

Giving birth had clearly drained much of her strength, and when she finished, she was tired and hungry. The only thing to eat was what was in the bundles, and Marina steeled herself.

"I'm not doing it for myself," she said, addressing the cube of black space in the center of which she was standing on all fours. "It's for the children."

In the first bundle Marina found Nikolai's thigh, still in its blood-caked green trouser leg. With her sharp mandibles Marina ripped open the trouser leg along the line of red braid and peeled it off like sausage skin. Nikolai's thigh had a tattoo on it, jolly red ants holding cards sitting at a table with a tall, narrow-necked bottle. Marina thought about how she hadn't really had time to learn anything about her husband, and then she took a small bite of the thigh.

Nikolai tasted just as melancholy and thorough as he had been in life, and Marina burst into tears. She remembered his strong, resilient front legs, covered in sparse red stubble, and the way they had touched her body, which had brought her only incomprehensible boredom, now seemed full of warmth and tenderness. Marina fought her depression by reading the scraps of newspaper lying on the floor in front of her.

"There is no strength left even for indignation," wrote an unknown author. "One can only marvel at the shameless behavior of the Masons from the infamous lodge P-4 (Psychoanalysis-4), who have mocked international public opinion for many decades and even taken their barbarous effrontery so far as to place the two grossest obscenities of the ancient Coptic language, which the Masons use for vilifying the most sacred objects of others' national culture, at the center of an international scientific polemic. The two phrases in question are 'sigmund freud' and 'eric berne,' which in translation mean 'stinking goat' and 'erect wolf's penis.' When will the science of Magadan, the last truly Nordic science, shake off the years of torpor and straighten up its mighty shoulders?"

Marina couldn't understand what this was all about. She could guess that the article came from an entire world of the arts and sciences which she knew nothing about but which she had glimpsed in passing on the poster stand by the seashore. It was a world populated by smiling, broad-shouldered men holding logarithmic slide rules and books, by children gazing dreamily into a distance invisible to adults, by impossibly beautiful women, frozen at their drawing boards and pianos in anxious anticipation of happiness. Marina was bitter that she would never find her own way to this world, but her children might, and she felt concerned for the eggs lying in the recess. She crawled over to them and studied them carefully.

Their dull skins had become semitransparent, and she could see the embryos. They were really nothing like ants and reminded her more of fat worms, but the vague outline of their future form was visible. Five of them were sexless workers, but the sixth and the seventh had wings, and Marina felt a shock of happiness and alarm when she saw that one of them was a boy and the other was a girl. She went back to the bed and collected some straw, which she carefully packed around the eggs. Then she took off the curtain and covered them with it. She tunneled into the remaining pile of straw. It pricked her naked body unpleasantly, but she tried not to pay attention to this inconvenience. For a while she gazed tenderly at the nest she had made. Then her eyes closed and she began to dream of the science of Magadan, straightening its shoulders under the black sky of the Arctic Ocean.

The next morning she noticed that although she hadn't eaten for a long time she had grown so fat that she couldn't possibly get out into the corridor, and she fitted into the chamber only because she was lying across it diagonally, with her head toward the clutch of eggs. She found it hard to believe that once she had been able to squeeze through the tiny square opening of the passageway in the wall. The folds of fat on her neck prevented her from even moving her head properly to see what had happened to her, but she could sense that below her neck there was a large, self-sufficient body living its own life, and it was no longer Marina at all. All that was left of Marina was a head with a few scattered thoughts and one pair of legs which still obeyed the head (the others were pinned against the floor by the body's abdomen). Vital juices were fomenting in the body; its entrails gave out strange, magical noises; and without asking permission from Marina, it would sometimes contract or turn over from one side to the other. Marina thought it must be a matter of genes: all she had eaten since becoming a mother was Nikolai's thigh, and that not because she was really hungry but because she hadn't wanted it to spoil.

Days went by, until one morning she woke feeling hungry in a way she had never felt before. This was no longer the hunger of the skinny girl she had once been; it was the hunger of a huge mass of living cells, every one of which was squealing shrilly about how hungry it was. Marina gathered her resolve and reached for the second bundle, opened it, and found a bottle of champagne. At first she was delighted, because she hadn't tried any champagne in the theater and had often wondered what it tasted like, but then she realized that she had absolutely no food at all. She reached out to the clutch of eggs, picked out one in which a sexless worker was maturing, and before she had time to change her mind she sank her mandibles into the semitransparent covering with a crunch. The egg tasted good and it was very filling, and before Marina came to her senses and regained her self-control, she had eaten another three.

"Well," she thought, as she felt a belch of contentment rise to her throat, "at least someone will be left. Otherwise . . ."

Marina felt a strong desire for some champagne, and she opened the bottle. The cork popped, and at least a third of the contents gushed out on the floor as white foam. Marina was upset, but then she remembered that was the way it had been in the film, and that calmed her down. She didn't like the champagne very much, because all she could get into her mouth from the bottle was fizzy foam, which was difficult to swallow, but she drank it all anyway, threw the empty bottle into a corner, and began reading the newspaper it had been wrapped in. It was another issue of *Magadan Ant*, but not as interesting as the first one. Almost all of it was devoted to a report from the Magadan Conference of Sexual Minorities, and it bored her, but she did find Major Bugaev, the author of the article on motherhood, in a big group photograph.

Marina put down the newspaper and began listening to the sensations of her own body. She couldn't believe that this huge fat mass was her. Or rather, this huge fat mass didn't believe that it was Marina.

"Tomorrow I'll start working out," thought Marina, feeling a bubble of hope rising up from her belly. "I'll get thin and I'll dig a way out to the south, to the sea . . . And I'll find that general who praised Nikolai. He'll marry me, and then . . ."

Marina was afraid to think any further than that. But she

felt she was still young and full of strength, and if she didn't give up, she could easily start all over again. Then she fell asleep and slept for a very long time, without any dreams.

She was wakened by a chomping sound. She opened her eyes and froze in horror. Two wide expressionless eyes were watching her from the corner. Immediately below the eyes were two sharp and powerful jaws, which were rapidly grinding something to a pulp, and below them was a small, worm-like white body covered with short, springy scales.

"Who are you?" Marina asked in fright.

"I'm your daughter, Natasha," the creature replied.

"What are you eating?" asked Marina.

"Eggs," Natasha mumbled innocently.

"Ah . . ."

Marina glanced at the recess where the eggs had been and saw that it was empty. She turned a gaze of reproach on Natasha.

"What can we do, Ma?" Natasha said, with her mouth full. "That's the way life is. If Andryusha had hatched first, he would have eaten me."

"What Andryusha?"

"My brother," said Natasha. "He said to me, let's wake up our ma. Straight out of the egg he said it to me. But I said, if you were first to break through the egg skin, would you wake up our ma? He didn't say anything, so I . . ."

"Oh, Natasha, how could you?" Marina whispered, shaking her head as she scrutinized her daughter. She was no longer thinking about the eggs; all her feelings were overwhelmed by the amazing awareness that this strange creature that moved and talked so naturally was her own daughter. Marina remembered the wooden poster kiosk near the videobar, with its images of an unattainably happy life, and mentally she tried to place Natasha in it.

Natasha looked at her without speaking, and then asked: "What's wrong, Ma?"

"Nothing," said Marina. "I'll tell you what, Natasha. Go

down the corridor and you'll find an accordion. Bring it back here, but be careful. Don't let the cover on the door fall in."

A few minutes later Natasha returned with a black box emanating bitter cold.

"Now listen, Natasha," said Marina. "My life has been terribly hard, and so was your late father's. I want everything to be different for you. But life is complicated."

Marina wondered how to squeeze into a few words all her bitter experience, all the thoughts she'd had through the long nights, so that Natasha would grasp the point.

"Life," she began, remembering very distinctly the triumphant smile on the face of the ugly bitch wrapped in her lemon-colored curtain, "is a struggle, and the strongest win. I want you to win, Natasha. Beginning today, you're going to learn to play your father's accordion."

"What for?" asked Natasha.

"You'll become a performer," Marina explained, nodding toward the dark hole in the wall, "and you'll work in the Magadan Military Opera House. It's a fine life, pure and joyful"—Marina recalled the general with his worn mandibles and paralyzed facial muscles—"and you meet all kinds of remarkable people. Do you want to live like that? To go to France?"

"Yes," Natasha said softly.

"Good," said Marina. "Then let's get started."

Natasha made astonishing progress. In a few days she learned to play so well that Marina decided she must have inherited her father's talent. The only musical score they found in the *Magadan Ant* was for the song "On Guard Over the Sea," which was presented as an example of genuine Magadan art. Natasha began playing it right away, reading the notes, and Marina listened in astonishment to the roaring of the waves and the howling of the wind as they fused into a hymn to the indomitable will of an ant who overcame the elements. She wondered what fate had in store for her daughter.

"What a beautiful song," she whispered as she watched Natasha's fingers flit over the keyboard.

Marina tried to remember the melody from the French film, humming it for her daughter as best she could. Natasha picked up the motif immediately, played it a few times, then thought about it and played it differently, and Marina remembered that was how it actually had been in the film. After that, she had complete faith in her daughter, and when Natasha fell asleep beside her, she covered the defenseless white sausage of her body with the blanket as though Natasha was still an egg.

Sometimes in the evening they would dream of how Natasha would become a famous performer and Marina would come to her concerts, sit in the front row, and in the end give way to a proud mother's tears. Natasha loved planning the concerts: she would sit on a box in front of her mother, pressing the accordion to her chest and playing "On Guard Over the Sea," or "Midnight in Moscow." At the most unexpected moments, Marina would interrupt her playing with a shrill cry of "bravo," clapping furiously with the two limbs that still obeyed her. Then Natasha would get up and bow, and it was as though she had never done anything else in her life. Marina had to wipe away the tears with a handful of straw. She felt that she was living through Natasha, and all she needed from life now was happiness for her daughter.

But the days went by, and Marina began to notice a strange lethargy in the girl. Sometimes Natasha would suddenly stop playing and sit there without moving, staring fixedly at the wall.

"What's wrong, daughter?" Marina would ask.

"Nothing," Natasha would reply, and start playing again.

Sometimes she would put down the accordion and crawl into a part of the chamber where Marina couldn't see her. At these times she wouldn't answer any questions, and Marina didn't know what she was doing. Sometimes her friends came visiting, but Marina never saw them; she only heard their young, confident voices.

One day Natasha asked her: "Ma, who has the best life, ants or flies?"

"Flies," answered Marina. "But only for a short while."

"And after that short while?"

"Let me think how to put it." Marina pondered. "Of course, they have quite a good life, but it's superficial, and they can't put any confidence in the future."

"Do you have any confidence in the future?"

"Me? Of course I do. Where could I go, except for here?"

Natasha pondered. "And do you have any confidence in my future?" she asked.

"Yes," replied Marina, "don't you worry, my dear."

"Can you manage not to have any?"

"What?" asked Marina.

"Can you manage not to be sure about anything to do with me?"

"Why do you want me to?"

"Why, why! Because as long as you have confidence in my future, I'll never get out of here either."

"Why, you ungrateful creature," Marina shouted angrily. "I've given you everything, devoted my life to you, and you . . ."

She swung her hand at Natasha, but her daughter crawled quickly away to her corner.

"Natasha," Marina called after a while. "Natasha, can you hear me?"

But Natasha didn't answer. Marina decided that her daughter had taken offense, and she decided to leave her in peace. She lowered her head and fell asleep. The next morning she was surprised not to feel Natasha's small rubbery body beside hers.

"Natasha!" she called.

Nobody answered.

"Natasha!" Marina called again, shifting uneasily on the bed.

Natasha didn't respond, and Marina fell into a panic. She tried to turn over, but the immensely fat body wouldn't obey her. She had the sudden idea that perhaps it was still capable of moving but simply didn't understand what Marina wanted, or couldn't decode the signals the brain was sending its muscles. Marina made a tremendous effort of will, but the body's only response was a quiet gurgling somewhere deep in its entrails. Marina tried again, and her head turned a little, so she could see the other corner of the chamber, and by turning her eyes as far as she could, she made out a small silvery cocoon hanging from the ceiling. It looked to her as though it was made of numerous layers of fine silk thread.

"Natasha," she called again.

"What, Ma?" said a small quiet voice inside the cocoon.

"What's all this?" Marina asked.

"It's obvious," answered Natasha. "I'm pupating. It's time."

"Pupating?" Marina repeated, and burst into tears. "Why didn't you call me? Are you completely grownup now?"

"Seems like it," replied Natasha. "I'll decide things for myself from now on."

"What are you going to do when you hatch out?" asked Marina.

"I'm going to be a fly," Natasha said from the ceiling.

"You're joking!"

"No, I'm not. I don't want to live like you, don't you get it?"

"Natasha darling, my little one," wailed Marina, "come to your senses! There's never been such a disgrace in our family!"

"Well, there will be now," Natasha said calmly.

•

The next morning Marina was awakened by a squeaking sound. The cocoon hanging from the ceiling was swaying slightly, and Marina realized that Natasha was ready to hatch out.

"Natasha," Marina began, trying to speak calmly, "you must understand. In order eventually to have freedom and sunshine, you have to work hard all your life. It's impossible otherwise. The road you're going to follow leads to the bottom of life, where no one can save you. Do you understand?"

The cocoon split lengthwise, and a head appeared in the top of the opening. It was Natasha, but she was nothing like the little girl who had spent long evenings playing Magadan concerts with Marina.

"Where do we live, then, up at the top?" she asked rudely.

"Just you wait," Marina threatened. "You'll come back here in rags with your eggs in the hem of your skirt, and I won't let you in the door."

"Don't bother," said Natasha.

She had already split open the wall of the cocoon, and instead of a modest ant's body, Marina saw a typical young fly in a short sexy dress with spangles. Of course, Natasha was beautiful, but not with the chaste and rapidly exhausted beauty of an ant female. She looked extremely vulgar, but there was something enchanting and attractive in her vulgarity, and Marina realized that if the fleshy-faced man from the French film had had to choose between the young Marina and Natasha, he would certainly have chosen Natasha.

"You whore!" Marina screeched, feeling female jealousy mingling with her offended maternal passions.

"Whore yourself," replied Natasha, without turning around. She was fixing her hair.

"You . . . Why, you . . ." muttered Marina. "Talking like that to your mother . . . Get out of my house! Do you hear me, get out!"

"I'm going anyway," said Natasha, finishing her hair. "I've got to get out quick."

"Immediately," shouted Marina. "Using words like that to your mother! Get out!"

"And I'm sick of your accordion, you old fool," Natasha flung at Marina. "Play it yourself. I hope it kills you."

Marina dropped her head back onto the straw, sobbing loudly. She was expecting that after a few minutes Natasha would come to her senses and crawl back to apologize, and she even decided not to forgive her right away but make her suffer a while, when she heard the sound of a trowel slicing into the earth.

"Natasha!" she shouted, turning her head with an incredible effort. "What are you doing?"

"Nothing," said Natasha. "Just digging my way out."

"The way out's over there. Do you want to destroy everything your father and I built?"

Natasha didn't answer. She went on digging with furious concentration, not even turning around, despite the curses which Marina flung at her head.

Then Marina leaned her head over as close as she could to the black hole in the wall and shrieked: "Help! Help! Anybody! Police!"

The only reply was the distant howl of an icy wind.

"Help! Save me!" Marina called out again.

"What are you shouting for?" Natasha asked from the ceiling. "In the first place, there's nobody out there, and they couldn't hear you even if there was."

Marina realized that her daughter was right, and she slumped into an indifferent haze. Up near the ceiling the trowel scraped regularly against the earth for an hour or two, and then a ray of sunlight fell into the chamber, which was invaded by the long-forgotten smell of fresh air. Marina breathed in and realized that the world she thought had disappeared forever along with her youth was really very close at hand—and now it was almost autumn there, but it would still be warm and dry for a while.

"Bye, Ma," said Natasha.

"She's leaving me," Marina knew suddenly, and she shouted again: "Natasha! At least take the handbag!"

"Thanks," Natasha shouted back down. "I already have."

She covered the hole she had dug, and once again the chamber was dark and cold, but the few seconds of sunshine were enough for Marina to recall how things had been on that distant day when she walked along the boardwalk and life murmured from the sea, whispered in the leaves, and spoke from the sky, from the horizon, promising something wonderful.

Marina looked at the pile of newspapers and realized sadly that this was all she had left—or, rather, all that life had left for her. She was no longer offended at her daughter's behavior, and all she hoped was that Natasha would have better luck on the boardwalk. Marina knew that her daughter would come back, but she also knew that no matter how close Natasha might be to her, there would always be a subtle but opaque wall between them, as though the space in which they used to play at Magadan concerts had suddenly been divided from floor to ceiling by a yellow curtain.

THE SECOND WORLD

". . . to rid himself of the feeling," said Mitya, standing with his eyes closed in the center of the ledge under the shaft of the beacon, "that he was digging through space with his wings, and trying with all his might to suppress the realization that he'd been doing that all his life. As he flew with hundreds of other cicadas toward the distant mountain, for the second time in his life seeing the world as it really was, it suddenly grew dark, and he began to think he'd lost his way (although he didn't know exactly where he was going), but then he remembered that he was standing between two dark black-thorn bushes and the fantastic forms of weathered rocks projecting from the ground, which looked from where he was standing like patches of the sky without any stars."

He blinked several times and pressed his fingers against his eyelids. There was a weak bluish light behind them, but the blue point of light that had been shining there a few minutes before had disappeared.

"It's finished. I can't see anything anymore," he said. "How long did all that last?"

Dima shrugged.

"All right," said Mitya. "I understand."

"Cicadas are close relatives of ours," said Dima, "but they live in a completely different world. I'd call them underground moths. Everything down there is just the same as up here, but there isn't any light at all. So when they decide where they want to fly, they have to trust what others say."

He turned and set off up the path. Mitya followed him, and a minute or two later they emerged onto a flat area between the rocks, which ended on one side in empty space. From here they could see the sea and the broad track of moonlight stretching across it. There was a flickering glow down on the shoreline, too.

"Strange," said Mitya. "It's as though everything we try so hard to get back to all our lives never really went away at all. As though someone blindfolds us and we stop seeing it."

"Do you want to know who?"

"Yes," answered Mitya.

"Good," said Dima. "Because you're going to, anyway."

Mitya shuddered.

"What do you mean, I'm going to, anyway?"

"You see," said Dima, "your recent activities have disturbed an extremely powerful being. He doesn't like what's going on. And now he will come for you."

"What does he want from me?" Mitya asked.

"He believes that you are totally in his power. That you belong to him. What you are trying to do is a threat to his power, and this being will attack at any minute."

"Who is he?"

"A corpse," answered Dima, as though it was absolutely obvious.

"Whose corpse?"

"Yours," said Dima. "When I say 'corpse,' I mean that what's waiting for you is the being that lives instead of you. It seems to me that the very worst thing that can happen to you is for him to go on living for you. But if he dies, then you will live, and not him."

"Who is it that lives instead of me?" asked Mitya. "And how can a corpse die?"

"All right," said Dima. "He doesn't live for you, his deadness replaces your life. That's all words, it doesn't matter. Talking about it is useless, anyway. Go and see for yourself."

"What about you?" asked Mitya.

"You're the only one who can actually meet him," said Dima. "And everything that happens from now on depends on you."

"Do I have to go back into the bushes?" asked Mitya. "How many more times?"

"I don't know where he'll find you. But he's already here. Very close."

"Where?" Mitya asked, scared.

Dima laughed and said nothing. He walked over to the edge of the rocks, almost as far as the drop into the sea, and turned away, as though he didn't want anything to do with what was happening behind him.

Mitya looked around. The rocks on all sides had the most varied shapes. On some of them there were tufts of grass that rustled in the wind, making it seem as though the rocks themselves were rustling. From behind, Dima's motionless figure also seemed like a dark outcrop of rock.

There was nothing else on the ledge. Mitya went over to the path they had just walked along and began descending, clutching at the bushes and the stones. The last time, he had been following Dima and he didn't realize how hard it was to walk here. Somehow it had seemed lighter then. Now that the moon was behind the rocky crest, he had to feel with his foot for the next stone, and grope for branches to hang on to. After a few feet of this, Mitya felt as though he was suspended in dark space, clinging to a few rocks projecting out of nowhere, without the slightest guarantee that there would be any further support ahead. He froze.

"Where am I going?" he thought. "And why?"

He closed his eyes and tried to focus on his own sensations

and thoughts, but there were none. It was simply dark, cool, and still. He could go on down the path or back to the ledge where he had left Dima. There didn't seem to be any real difference between the two courses of action.

Mitya tried taking one more step, and a stone rolled over under his shoe. He almost went tumbling after it, but at the last second he managed to grab a thorny branch, which left deep scratches on his palm. The stone bounced against the cliff face, then hurtled into the rustling bushes, and again there was silence.

"What's happening to me?" Mitya thought, licking his palm. "Why am I standing God knows where in total darkness waiting for my own corpse? Is this where I've gotten to by flying toward the light? This isn't what I was looking for. Maybe I don't know what it is—but it's not this, that's for sure."

The wind blew, and down below the invisible grass rustled.

"I'll go back now and tell him I've had enough . . . Who does he think he is, anyway? Where did he come from? On the other hand, of course, that's a meaningless question. From the same place as me. And what he says is right, and I always knew it anyway, without him. And I knew all sorts of other things as well . . . Where has it all gone?"

Mitya tried to recall the other things, and a few fragmentary pictures appeared in front of his eyes, almost the same way as in the well, like a film made up of separate exposures. The best things turned out to be the simplest, the kind you could never tell anyone about. They were the moments when life suddenly acquired meaning—and it even became clear that it had never really lost it; rather, that *Mitya* had lost it. But he couldn't understand the reason for the meaning suddenly becoming clear again, and the snapshots that followed through his memory were quite different from each other. For instance, strips of light across a ceiling at night, looking like the beams of spotlights trying in vain to pick out the lamp on the ceiling, or the view from a dusty train window of a deep expanse of evening sky stretching back into a forest cutting, or a few unpolished bottle-green emeralds lying on the palm of his hand. The strange and inexpressible knowledge linked with these things had disappeared, and what was left in his memory was more like the wrapper from a piece of candy eaten by some being that had lived inside him for a long time, imperceptibly existing in his each and every thought (the thoughts seemed to be its habitat), but always concealing itself from view.

Mitya realized that this was the being which had been chewing on him for most of his life and had almost devoured him completely. This time, it hadn't had enough time to hide. This was his corpse.

But there was nothing he could do about it, unless he picked up a rock and hit himself over the head.

Once again, Mitya felt the dark emptiness below him with his foot. Then he turned and began scrambling back up the hill. It was simpler to climb up, and in a minute he was back in the bright moonlight on the ledge.

Dima was standing in the same spot, in the same pose, still quite motionless, and Mitya felt annoyed at what he thought was melodramatic behavior.

"I understand now," he said. "I understand what you were talking about. Hey."

He slapped Dima on the shoulder, and Dima slowly turned around.

But it wasn't Dima.

It was the being of whose existence Mitya had had an intimation just a minute earlier. There could be no mistake, although Mitya could not say why he was so sure. But at the very instant when he saw before him his own face, blue and exhausted, he remembered a passage from an old Japanese book where a man has a nightmare in which he is running along the seashore, trying to escape from his own self, risen up out of the grave. Now the same thing was happening to him, but there was no grave, the seashore was far below, and this was no dream that he could wake from.

Mitya staggered back, and the corpse stepped after him. Mitya dashed for the path leading down, but when he thought of himself clutching the branches again, he slowed down and paused for a moment, trying to decide which way to run. Then he felt his own hand grasp him by the shoulder.

With a slow, caricature movement from some sanitized horror movie, the corpse raised its hands and took Mitya by the throat, and Mitya felt himself also choking somebody. He squeezed with all the strength in his fingers and knew that in another second he would suffocate. He drew back his hands, and the fingers on his throat simultaneously relaxed.

"I get it," Mitya thought. He turned around and raised his foot to take a step, then felt his own hand catch him by the left shoulder again. He felt a momentary surge of fury, lashed out at the corpse with his foot, and when he came to his senses, he was down on all fours. He stood up, wheezing the air into his reluctant lungs. It was very difficult, not just because he couldn't catch his breath after the blow, but also because the corpse's fingers once again closed on his throat in mindless determination, and in order to take a breath, he had to slacken his own grip on that cold blue throat. Mitya made one more attempt to escape from the corpse's clutches, but although his movements were quick and powerful and the corpse moved extremely slowly, he failed.

"Well? How long are we going to stand here like this?" asked Mitya. The corpse didn't answer. Looking closer, Mitya saw that its eyelids were open slightly and it seemed to be looking down. The corpse was breathing very slightly, and it seemed to Mitya it was trying to remember something.

"Hey, you!" Mitya called.

"Wait a moment," said the corpse, and went on breathing quietly.

"Perhaps," thought Mitya, "I should simply strangle him? And put up with it myself for a little while?"

He began breathing in carefully, trying to gather enough air into his lungs, but he felt the corpse's fingers crushing his throat, and every second their pressure grew stronger. Mitya tried to pull the cold fingers from his throat, but that didn't help. The corpse seemed to have decided to strangle him first. Mitya was seriously frightened, and the corpse's fingers on his throat immediately relaxed in confusion.

"No," thought Mitya, "that's not the way. Perhaps I should try crossing him, just in case? It can't make things any worse."

The corpse suddenly freed one hand, crossed Mitya with it hastily, and grabbed him by the throat again.

"That's no good," thought Mitya, and then he finally realized that *he* wasn't thinking what he was thinking, the corpse was.

"Hey," he heard Dima's voice call from somewhere above. "How much longer are you going to go on waltzing with him?"

Mitya looked up. Dima was sitting on a tall rock a short distance to the right, his legs dangling over the edge, as he watched the languid struggle going on below.

"Kick him in the balls," he advised, "and then a double fist to the back of the neck."

"What shall I do with him?" Mitya muttered.

"I don't know," said Dima. "It's your corpse, not mine. Do anything you like. It's in your hands."

For a few more minutes Mitya stood looking into the corpse's face. There was nothing frightening about it; it was calm, weary, and sad, as though the corpse was not holding his throat but rather the handrail on the metro he was riding home on from some stale and boring job.

"If, God forbid, this happened to me," Dima finally said from his rock, "the very first thing I would do would be to take a close look at just who I have in front of me."

Mitya took another look at the corpse's weary face and spotted a very faint frown of sadness and resentment, the shadow of some dream that never came true. And instead of revulsion and terror, he felt genuine pity for his corpse; as soon as that happened, the cold fingers once again tightened on his throat, but this time Mitya felt it was some external force choking him, and he could do nothing to slacken the grip. He kicked the corpse's shinbone with all his might, but all he did was bruise his toe: he might as well have kicked a pillar of salt. Colored stripes and spots appeared in front of his eyes, he knew he was about to lose consciousness, and that when it had strangled him, the corpse would go home to read Marcus Aurelius.

Then his attention was caught by one of the spots of color dancing in front of his eyes. In fact, the small blue spot was not dancing but remained perfectly still, which was why Mitya noticed it. It was the same blue point of light which had disappeared after he had focused it on the cicada. Mitya realized that he could use it again. He looked at the exhausted blue face in front of him, and he felt that his fingers were no longer clutching a throat but something soft and slightly damp.

On the ground in front of him stood a large sphere of dung, and his arms were sunk in it almost to the elbows.

He pulled his arms out, shook them several times in disgust, and turned to face Dima, who had jumped down from his rock and come over to the sphere.

"What is it?" asked Mitya.

"As if you didn't know," said Dima. "It's a ball of dung."

It was true. Mitya did know what it was, and he knew very well what to do with it.

"How much you have stolen from me," he thought, gazing at the sphere in hatred. "You stole absolutely everything there could be."

Then he realized that once again it was not him thinking, but the sphere. In fact, there was nothing that could be stolen from him, and there was really nothing much for him to think about. He lifted his foot, about to kick the huge mound of dung, but he realized in time that there was no one there to kick, and that made him angrier than anything else. He pushed against the surface of the sphere, carefully, so that his hand wouldn't sink into it. It began to shift surprisingly easily, and he rolled it to the edge of the cliff and pushed it over.

The sphere traveled a few feet over the steep slope, then bounced off it and disappeared from sight. A few long moments later, Mitya heard a loud splash.

Mitya looked around. Dima was nowhere to be seen. Then he noticed a faint flickering light in a wide crack between two protruding rocks, and he thought Dima must be there. He walked over to the crack and clicked his cigarette lighter. Holding the flame out in front of him, he stepped over a stone that was like a doorstep. The protruding rocks came together above his head, forming a sort of deep cave.

Ahead of him Mitya saw a faint light, as though Dima was holding a dying match in his hand, and he called again: "Dima! Where are you?"

The other person didn't answer.

"Who are you?" Mitya shouted and walked on.

The light moved to meet him, and a few steps later the hand held out in front of him with the rapidly heating lighter struck unexpectedly against the mirror in the heavy semicircular frame of dark wood.

ENTOMOPILOGUE

"So what I want to do, Pasha," Sam said to Arnold in a thin tenor, "is go across and pick up some wheels, and then come back under my own steam. Then I sell the wheels here, Pasha, and for big money. They're very pricey these days. And then with what I make on the deal I have the bread for another two new ones."

Sam was sitting at the beginning of the boardwalk with his legs dangling over the edge of a wooden fence. His fingers were pressed so hard into the plastic sides of his briefcase that the nails were white, and his face, covered with tiny beads of sweat, bore an expression of intense concentration. He was looking toward the sea, but what he saw was obviously something quite different.

"Of course, I do it all in bucks," he continued. "Not like the jerks who've sold all their stuff and got stuck with rubles. You know what a good thing I'm on to, Pasha. By the way, do you want a hunting license?"

"What for?" Arnold asked.

"So you can hang a gun on the wall and it's official. When they come to rob your apartment, you take it down and . . .

Just think about it, Pasha. Real security, eh? I'm getting one for myself, you have to go to four different offices and pay bribes every time you call. Costs about twenty-five hundred by the time you've finished. And there's this other idea I've got . . . Why don't you come to Hungary with me? The ticket's sixty dollars, pricey all right, but it's worth it. And you think about that gun, that's real power in your hands . . ."

Arnold shook him by the shoulder. "Sam," he said, "pull yourself together."

Sam shuddered, then shook his head and looked around him. He opened his case, spat something red into a glass jar, and put it back in its place.

"That's a bit more interesting," he said in his usual voice. "At least I can see how something could be made of that."

Suddenly Sam and Arnold glanced up at a low buzzing sound from the direction of the sea. They saw a wasp—a very rare insect in the Crimea—approaching the wall, dressed in a dark double-breasted suit and clutching a small Bible in his hand. His lips were extended in a wide, joyless smile, and the sun gleamed pitilessly on his white teeth. The wasp came closer and spoke quietly to Sam in English, pointing off to the right with a hand weighed down by a heavy gold Rolex watch.

"Oh, God," said Sam. "I knew it."

He jumped down on the grass and waited for Arnold to go through the complicated maneuver of shifting his balance, turning the full weight of his fat body a hundred and eighty degrees, and hanging from the wall by his hands.

"If you want my opinion," said Arnold, landing heavily on the grass, "in these situations you have to be tough from the very beginning. Otherwise, it only means both sides suffer more. Never give them any reason to hope for anything."

Sam said nothing. They started walking on the boardwalk, heading in silence toward the open-air café.

A small crowd had gathered by one of the tables, and a single glance was enough to see that something unpleasant had happened. Sam turned pale and ran on ahead. Elbowing aside the idle spectators, he squeezed his way through, and then froze.

Hanging from the edge of the table, swaying in the wind, was a strip of flypaper. There were several small leaves and bits of paper stuck to it, and in the very center, with her head slumped forward in exhaustion, was Natasha. Her wings were stuck flat against the surface, and they were suffused with its poisonous slime. One of them stuck out to the side, and the other stuck up at an indecent angle. The dark circles under her closed eyes covered half her face, and the green dress that had captivated Sam with its bright sheen had turned dull and was covered in brown spots.

"Natasha!" Sam cried, dashing toward her. "Natasha!"

They held him back. Natasha opened her eyes, saw Sam, and straightened the fringe of hair on her forehead in a gesture of alarm. The effort was obviously too much for her, and her exhausted hand dropped and stuck in the poisonous glue.

"Sam," she said, opening her mouth with a tremendous effort, "it's good that you came. See how . . ."

"Natasha," Sam whispered, "forgive me."

"Imagine, Sam," Natasha said softly, "I was practicing in front of the mirror, like a real fool. 'Please, cheese and pepperoni.' I thought I would go away with you . . ."

Borne on the wind from the speaker at the boat station came the faint trilling of balalaikas.

"You understand, Sam, not to America, but with you . . . I was afraid that when I was there I . . . Do you remember how we went swimming? And, you know, my mother even sewed me a new dress out of her curtain. She kept saying, 'Natasha, play the accordion for me, soon you'll be going away forever' . . . Don't tell her anything . . . Let her just think I went without saying goodbye . . ."

Natasha lowered her head, and small teardrops glistened on her eyelashes.

"Look out," said a bass female voice from the left. "Let me through there."

The waitress with the crimson ringworm on a face as dour

as fate went up to the table. She was carrying an immense aluminum pan with the inscription "III section" in red. She set the pan on the ground, shook the leftovers from the plates on the table into it, and then with a single movement of her powerful and cruel hand she tore the strip of flypaper with Natasha on it from the table, crumpled it up into a small ball, and threw it in as well. Once again Sam was restrained by the hands of strangers. The waitress attached a fresh strip of flypaper to the table, picked up the pan, and moved on to the next one. The people gathered there began to disperse, but Sam remained rooted to the spot, his eyes fixed on the strip of sticky yellow paper dangling from the table.

"Let's go, Sam," he heard Arnold's soft voice say. "You can't do anything to help her now. Let's go. You need a drink, that's what you need. Let's go to Arthur's place, he's moved into poor old Archibald's house. He's put in two big tanks and a fax. It's comfortable and quiet there. Just stop looking at the flypaper, please, Sam . . ."

"Let me through, please."

Sam looked up and saw a strange figure dressed in something like a silver cloak, its edge trailing along the ground— or perhaps it was a pair of long heavy wings folded on his back.

"Let me through, please," the figure repeated. "And if you're feeling sad, try rereading page 51."

Sam stepped aside.

•

The large sphere of dung, which was an unusual reddish color, tumbled aside, and the long empty boardwalk opened up ahead of Dmitry. In the distance there was a deck chair, and reclining on it was another sphere of dung. When the deck chair was closer, it became clear that the sphere of dung was a fat red ant in a navy uniform. His sailor's hat bore an inscription in gold letters, *Ivan Krilov*, and his chest was a veritable garden of ribbons and medals, in numbers that could only have sprouted after the fabric of his tunic had been fertilized with the dung of a long and senseless life. He was holding an open tin can in one hand while he licked the salt water from an American humanitarian-aid sausage held in the other. On the wall in front of him was a portable television with a white pennant tied to its aerial. On the screen a dragonfly was dancing in the crossed beams of several searchlights.

A cold wind sprang up, and the ant raised the collar of his tunic and leaned forward. The dragonfly hopped up and down a few times, straightened her beautiful long wings, and began to sing.

The back of the ant's head, where the black ribbons with the faded anchors fluttered in the wind, began flushing dark blood-red. Dmitry walked on.

The sea murmured quietly and the sun glimmered through the green screen of the cypresses which grew along the road. The boardwalk ahead was empty except for a single strange figure, half walking, half dancing toward him.

As he came closer, Dmitry could see it was a young boy whose eyes were red from crying. He was moving slowly, throwing his arms out ahead of him at every step, as though he was pushing along some intolerably heavy burden; even though there was nothing in front of him, he was breathing heavily, and his forehead was beaded with sweat.

" 'Scuse me," he said, "can you tell me where the beach is? Pa said I had to go there no matter what, but I can't see a thing in all this damn fog."

Moscow, 1993

FOR THE BEST IN PAPERBACKS, LOOK FOR THE

In every corner of the world, on every subject under the sun, Penguin represents quality and variety—the very best in publishing today.

For complete information about books available from Penguin—including Puffins, Penguin Classics, and Arkana—and how to order them, write to us at the appropriate address below. Please note that for copyright reasons the selection of books varies from country to country.

In the United Kingdom: Please write to *Dept. JC, Penguin Books Ltd, FREEPOST, West Drayton, Middlesex UB7 0BR.*

If you have any difficulty in obtaining a title, please send your order with the correct money, plus ten percent for postage and packaging, to *P.O. Box No. 11, West Drayton, Middlesex UB7 0BR*

In the United States: Please write to *Consumer Sales, Penguin USA, P.O. Box 999, Dept. 17109, Bergenfield, New Jersey 07621-0120.* VISA and MasterCard holders call 1-800-253-6476 to order all Penguin titles

In Canada: Please write to *Penguin Books Canada Ltd, 10 Alcorn Avenue, Suite 300, Toronto, Ontario M4V 3B2*

In Australia: Please write to *Penguin Books Australia Ltd, P.O. Box 257, Ringwood, Victoria 3134*

In New Zealand: Please write to *Penguin Books (NZ) Ltd, Private Bag 102902, North Shore Mail Centre, Auckland 10*

In India: Please write to *Penguin Books India Pvt Ltd, 706 Eros Apartments, 56 Nehru Place, New Delhi 110 019*

In the Netherlands: Please write to *Penguin Books Netherlands bv, Postbus 3507, NL-1001 AH Amsterdam*

In Germany: Please write to *Penguin Books Deutschland GmbH, Metzlerstrasse 26, 60594 Frankfurt am Main*

In Spain: Please write to *Penguin Books S. A., Bravo Murillo 19, 1° B, 28015 Madrid*

In Italy: Please write to *Penguin Italia s.r.l., Via Felice Casati 20, I-20124 Milano*

In France: Please write to *Penguin France S. A., 17 rue Lejeune, F-31000 Toulouse*

In Japan: Please write to *Penguin Books Japan, Ishikiribashi Building, 2-5-4, Suido, Bunkyo-ku, Tokyo 112*

In Greece: Please write to *Penguin Hellas Ltd, Dimocritou 3, GR-106 71 Athens*

In South Africa: Please write to *Longman Penguin Southern Africa (Pty) Ltd, Private Bag X08, Bertsham 2013*